Into the Deep Woods

Stories & Poems

Jonathan Arena

We understand the cost in our hearts
When fog rolls in and covers the sea
Studied all the maps and all the charts
We just needed the time to be free

Downstairs

Madeline lifted her head from the warm pillow and stared across the bedroom. Her eyes adjusted to the dark, and the silhouettes of stacked boxes soon sharpened.

The urge to unpack was strong but her mother insisted, rather shouted, that she get a good night's sleep before her first day of school. Not *the* first day. Only *her* first day. At a new school, in a new city, as far away from her father as her mother could afford.

She rested her head back down on the pillow, but now it felt cold. She flipped it over, but the other side was freezing. She sighed and just lay there.

Glass smashed somewhere in the house. Madeline sprang from the bed sheets and looked to the door. She had left it open in the hope that it would help her sleep, but that was never going to be the case. She could not remember where the nightlight was packed, but now more than ever she wished she had searched a little harder.

Her heart jumped from her chest when a second crash rang through the walls.

It came from downstairs.

She swung her feet to the side of the bed and tried to steady her breath. Inhaling and exhaling, inhaling and exhaling. But to no avail.

She slid off the bed and planted her bare feet on the hardwood floor. It was cold and foreign. Her last bedroom had carpet, and she preferred it. Moving one foot tentatively in front of the other, she approached the door and opened it wider. It screeched painfully against the old hinges.

Madeline stuck her head outside. The hallway seemed a darker shade of black than her bedroom. So dark she could not even see its end. She had no idea where the light switch rested on the wall either. More than likely, it hid behind a stack of boxes. No use in trying to find it in this dark, she thought.

She slipped her body out into the hall and took a few steps. After the crashes and the hinges, the silence now felt eerie and troubling.

She tiptoed toward the next door, toward her mother's bedroom. A dim light seeped out from underneath the closed door. She must already be up, perhaps even downstairs. Her heart slowed to a normal pace as more optimistic scenarios filled her imagination.

Her mother frequented the bathroom in the middle of the night and must have bumped into something, knocking it over and breaking it. It wouldn't be the first time. That must be it. But there was a bathroom upstairs, and what about the second crash?

Her mind drifted again to the gloomier possibilities.

She walked what seemed like a hundred yards to her mother's door, maneuvering past more boxes and plastic crates that crowded the dark hall.

She turned the knob and pushed it open.

Light from a single lamp on the ground blinded Madeline's eyes. She shielded them and moved beside the bed. Unpacked boxes and garbage bags of clothes filled the room and left only a narrow path.

Her mother snored with her mouth open, sprawled on a coverless mattress. She clutched a glass bottle of vodka with only a few drops left. An unlit cigarette was stuck to her bottom lip, and her eyelids flickered as if she was having a dream. Or maybe a nightmare.

"Mom?" Madeline seized the cigarette from her lip and placed it on the ground next to the lamp. She attempted to grab the bottle too but her mother's grip was too strong.

"Mom?" she repeated louder but her mother only shifted in position. Not even a gentle shake of her body garnered a reply.

The sound of smashing glass rang through the house a third time. Madeline snapped to attention and stared at the open door of her mother's bedroom. She swallowed.

"Wake up, please," she looked back to her mother, but had little hope of succeeding. Her mother snorted, mumbled and then snored louder.

Madeline sighed and made her way back to the doorway. She looked once more at her mother before leaving and entering the black of the hall.

Her night vision had been ruined by her

mother's lamp. She would have to start all over again. The end of the hall, beyond the lamp's reach, looked blacker than the bottom of the well at her last home. The one where her favorite doll fell and stayed alone until her father rescued the loyal companion the following day.

She crept down the rest of the hall, blindly moving her hands across the boxes that lined the path, relying on touch to find her way.

She made it to the stairwell leading downstairs. She took another deep breath and, barely able to see the next step, persisted downstairs with a rigid grip on the railing. The closer to the last step she moved, the louder the noise became. It was a scraping, scratching sound that hastened its pace, as if frustrated and impatient. Madeline's knees wobbled, but she held on to the railing even tighter and eventually reached the bottom.

She listened to the sounds, and her mind wandered to even darker places, focusing on one thing and one thing only.

Monsters.

She stood there. The darkness was thick, but she knew there was a light switch at the bottom of the stairs. She remembered her mother turning it on, so Madeline rubbed her hands along the surface of the wall, located the switch and flipped it. The ceiling light in the hallway illuminated to reveal even more boxes.

All noise ceased.

Madeline walked into the living room and turned on another light. Nothing except more boxes and unpositioned furniture. She stepped into the dining room and switched a third light on. More boxes.

No broken windows, no broken glass.

She began to wonder if she had imagined the whole thing. Her father always said she had a wild imagination. It was why he took her on so many trips to museums and parks. But he also said there were times and places to use it and times and places not to.

Uncertain, she continued.

Something dropped to the kitchen floor. Light scurrying of sharp claws against hard countertop. Madeline hesitated but could see the kitchen light switch from the hall's glow—she was almost there.

She closed her eyes and took another breath before proceeding. Eyes wide open again, straining against the darkness, she lunged for the switch. The kitchen burst into light, and Madeline locked eyes with the monster.

A raccoon.

The raccoon gazed into her eyes. Frozen at each other's presence, the two strangers remained tense and staring. The raccoon held a single cracker in his paws. His nose and whiskers twitched, and he began eating the cracker despite Madeline's watchful eye. A mess of crumbs rained down on the kitchen floor to join the box of crackers and shards of broken glass.

Madeline laughed suddenly. She laughed so hard she forgot all about the fear.

The raccoon finished the cracker in a flash. Madeline looked down to the floor, where the rest of the crackers rested. She stepped forward and carefully avoided the sharp glass. The raccoon jumped back and showed its teeth. Madeline stared into the animal's eyes once more and offered a gentle smile.

"It's okay, little guy. It's okay…"

She crept one more step toward the box and grabbed it from the floor. The raccoon snarled and studied her every move. Madeline's hand dove into the box and pulled out another cracker. She presented it to the raccoon, and its eyes lit up. It reached out with its paws and snatched the offering in a hurry. It retreated back into the corner, where sharp teeth made easy work of the dry cracker. More crumbs flew into the air and onto the floor.

Madeline's smile widened.

The raccoon never moved those piercing eyes from the girl. She even thought she saw a smile on the animal, but when the cracker was gone, the smile faded. It demanded more. And with little patience.

Madeline obliged.

When the box was empty of its contents, the animal demanded that too. It checked the box inside and out to make certain not a single crumb remained. When reality set in, the raccoon tossed the box to the floor and gazed upon Madeline with the eyes of a newborn puppy. The moment froze in time as the two species stared at one another.

SMASH.

A glass vodka bottle broke against the cabinets, and Madeline screamed. The startled raccoon rushed back out the open window and vanished into the black of the night. The window was not broken at all but wide open with no screen. The shattered glass was from the liquor bottles already piling up in the new house.

Madeline turned to the kitchen doorway to see her stumbling-drunk mother. The cigarette hung from her lips once more, and she fumbled with the lighter. The bags under her eyes looked like they weighed a ton.

"Get the hell outta here, ya damn rodent!" She finally lit the cigarette and puffed in perceived victory. "Damn thing, tryna break in my damn house. Mus' be related to ya father!" She laughed a wicked laugh.

Madeline closed her eyes and clenched her jaw.

"One of his stupid, no-good friends, I bet!" She laughed even harder, a villainous cackle. "Let me tell ya 'bout men like that, hon! Let me tell ya all 'bout those damn rodents!"

Madeline opened her eyes and looked down at all the broken glass on the floor. Her sense of fear flooded back in an instant. It surged through her body and crawled on her skin like a thousand spiders.

"Your father… That'll show 'em!" her mother rambled on. "Him and that damn cat! Son of a bitch. I hate cats! How the hell did it get in here? This is my house! My life!"

Madeline ignored her mother, as she had grown accustomed to doing over the last two years, and stared out the open window, where life seemed more promising, more optimistic.

Sunlight peeked over the horizon of the nearby hills and began peeling away the darkness outside.

Downstairs

Sunrays reached Madeline's nose and cheeks and warmed her face.

She smiled again, but only for a moment.

Spirits collapse and most turn back
Simple paths were never promised
Learning and evading the next attack
In the depths of the empty honest

Red Valley

Her eyes were beautiful. Bluer than the sky and deeper than the sea. The sunrise on her freckled cheeks intoxicated the young man.

"We should get married," he said.

Sorrow marred her face, and she slipped out of his hands. "You know we can't."

"Then let's run away." He gently raised her chin and gazed far back into her endless pupils where the entire world seemed captured.

"You know we can't do that either. Our families need us."

He laughed. "I'm the youngest of ten. My father doesn't need me. He's been telling me that my whole life. He only cares for his damn grapes."

"Well..." She looked back at the blades of grass. "Mine needs me."

The young man's focus strayed to the distance. Movement in the valley below snatched his attention and held it. Twelve knights on horseback traversed the narrow dirt road wedged between rows and rows of vineyards and the odd villa. They flew the King's Banner and trotted with confidence. Four of them held torches.

He stood for a better look. "They're early. The King's Games are not for three moons."

The young woman joined him and seemed even more surprised. Almost stunned. "Where are the barrel wagons?"

Men and women abandoned their tasks in the vineyards to greet the riding knights, but the armored men paid them no mind. They rode directly to the young woman's home, where four unmounted and approached. The other eight rode on.

Her father, mother and eldest brother met the knights outside their home.

"My father must be fuming that they went to your house first." The young man smirked. "Making better wine than your family has always been his life's work."

He spotted his own father emerging from his vines to see what was happening. And, as the young man predicted, his father did not seem pleased at the revelation. The young man chuckled.

"I don't like this." The young woman stepped forward. "It seems off. Why do they have torches?"

"They must have traveled through the night. The King must have orders for the wines."

"The torches look new."

"Second ones of the night. It was dark not too long ago, my love."

The head knight chatted with her father for a moment and then glanced back to the others with a simple nod.

Time seemed to stop. Silence filled the valley.

The young man and woman watched the scene unfold as time sped back up. And in one swift movement, the knight unsheathed a small blade and drove it into her father's chest.

"No!" she shouted.

The other knights drew their own swords and sliced her mother and brother down with ease. The young woman dashed down the slope, but the young man caught her and held her back. She struggled to break free.

"Let me go!" she screamed.

"So they can murder you too?" he shouted back. "We should go!"

"No!" She turned around and smacked him across the face. Shocked, he released his grip and watched her run down the valley slope alone.

Knights terrorized the neighboring vineyards in much the same manner. They sliced down laborers and set the vines ablaze.

Screams now filled the valley.

"Wait!" The young man sprinted after her.

He followed her down the slope and through her neighbor's vineyard. He followed her all the way to the front of the home, where she knelt crying in the pools of her family's blood.

"Father! Mother!" she hysterically sobbed over and over. But she paused when her mother faintly moved her hand onto hers.

"Mother…"

Blood dripped from her mother's lips as she tried to speak. No words found their way out, only more blood. Her hand went limp and her head fell sideways.

"No!" The young woman wept.

The young man approached with caution. She

cried harder and harder. He wanted to say something but had no idea what it should be.

A knight holding a torch exited her home. His gaze froze the young man like Medusa's glance. The knight's decorated armor appeared ill-fitted and the helmet too large. The moment lasted a lifetime.

The knight switched his gaze to the young woman. The young man's eyes followed. She remained beside the dead bodies.

"Get up!" The knight threw his torch inside the house and unsheathed a sword. He waved it in their direction and grew impatient. "I said, *get up!*"

The young man rushed to her side and pulled her away, but her clutch on her mother was strong. The knight stepped forward, and the young man finally yanked her free.

The tears worsened, and her anger shifted back at the young man, but at least they were running away. Into the vineyards and through the vines they went.

The knight gave chase but was clumsy in the heavy armor. The scraping of metal on the joints of the suit faded as they fled.

The young woman's legs collapsed in her continued hysteria. He did everything he could to pull her back up but only succeeded in dragging her across the tilled soil.

"Come on!" He looked around desperately. Her howling was certain to attract other knights. "We have to go! Come on!"

More crying, and the slow knight caught up. He did not look pleased at being put to such trouble. He readied his sword. "You little shits!"

"Come on!" the young man repeated. But she would not budge and held on to an old grapevine with all her strength. He tried everything, but she was not leaving these vines. He realized where they were. Her father's prized Pinot Noir surrounded them.

The young man looked to the ground in search of something. Anything. But he saw only rocky soil. Rocky soil. Rocks. He picked up a stone and threw it at the approaching knight. It struck his breastplate and surprised him enough to stop him in his tracks, but only for a moment.

The knight resumed his ungainly assault toward them with more determination. The young man picked up another rock and threw it. This one did nothing.

The knight lifted his sword and swung at the young man, but he dodged the blow. The knight was no swordsman at all but he swung again, this time cutting the young man's shoulder. The young man held the wound tightly, but blood seeped through his fingers and dripped down his arm.

The weeping from the young woman halted, and was replaced by a battle cry. The knight raised his sword, preparing for a killing blow on the young man when she attacked him from behind.

She jumped onto his back and threw off his helmet. She beat him over the head with her fists.

The knight was disoriented and swung wildly.

But he regained his senses and pushed his sword over his shoulder. The sharp blade slid into the young woman's eye socket. It pierced her brain and pushed blood out her ears and mouth.

Her screams were brief, and her blood spilled onto the ground like that of a gutted deer.

She dropped to the ground, lifeless.

The young man watched it all happen in an instant. She was alive one moment, dead the next. Dead.

The knight turned his attention back to the young man, but he only stared at the corpse.

She was dead.

The young man closed his eyes and accepted his fate. He would join her soon. He could even see her gorgeous smile behind his lids. And her eyes. Bluer than the sky and deeper than the sea.

The metallic thud of collapsing iron opened his eyes. The knight lay on the ground with an arrow sticking out of his forehead.

The young man turned to see his older brother lowering a short bow from his sights.

The young man moved slowly to the smaller of the two bodies. Blood trickled out her left eye socket, but the right was still open.

Open and staring back at him.

He broke the final gaze and never looked again. He couldn't. It ripped him apart.

His brother consoled him but quickly grew nervous. "Brother…"

The young man kept his face in his hands, tears spilling between his fingers. She was dead and would always be dead.

"Brother…"

The young man did not move. His body felt too heavy. His arms too sore, his legs too weary. And his shoulder was still bleeding, soaking his shirt in red. He dared not look at the wound, but he could feel its severity.

His brother grabbed his arm with so much force that he leapt up with a scream. He felt his wound stretch wider, and more blood flowed down his arm and chest. The pain jolted him to his feet, and he was now running with his brother. He looked behind him and saw the reason why.

Two more knights were headed their way.

They ran from one grape varietal to the next. One vineyard to the next. More screams filled the valley as families were slaughtered one at a time. Fathers, mothers, brothers, sisters, babies. The cries came from them all.

Black smoke reached the sky as vineyards and villas burned down. The smell of death overwhelmed them.

The two brothers looked up and saw that their home was still untouched. Not overtaken by knights, not on fire, no bodies. But then they saw it.

Three horses tied up outside, and a trail of blood.

The young man hesitated while his older brother followed the blood trail straight into the cellar. His brother disappeared inside with a notched arrow.

There was a shout, a quick struggle, and two knights stepped out with bloody swords.

The young man jumped behind the vines. The knights gazed around but did not see him. They lingered for a moment but soon sheathed their weapons and went back into the cellar.

He remembered the trailing knights. He turned

to see them coming around the corner in an awkward run. Their armor ill-fitting and helmets too big. The obvious became clearer and clearer.

These were no knights.

The young man remained underneath the vines one row away. The men had little practice in the armor. Their movements were clumsy and their eyesight in the helmet visor was poor.

The clanking of their steps came nearer and nearer until floundering right past without a clue of his presence.

They stopped before his home and gazed around in all directions. A shared glance and a shrug of confusion concluded their search.

Three men dressed as knights exited the cellar. The five of them congressed.

"That was the family? The one with the very special *King's* orders?"

They all laughed. "That was them."

"King's orders, that's rich."

"He was the King's favorite winemaker. His reds were showcased at the Games every year, lauded above all the others."

"Not anymore."

"No. Not anymore."

"Gives the name *Red Valley* a whole new meaning, eh?"

They laughed more.

"Lord, I cannot wait to get out of this armor!"

"Itchy, ain't it?"

"Hard to move too. Not sure how they do it."

"Good thing only peasants lived here."

"How about that one with the bow?"

"Not a bad shot. For a winemaking huntsman."

They laughed and strolled down to where the horses waited.

The young man moved from the vines and darted to the cellar. Smoke began to spill out of the entrance as he ran inside.

The cellar had rows and stacks of barrels lining the stone walls. Fire had consumed a section of it and was spreading quickly.

Nine slain bodies rested in a pile, with two more in front. The young man rubbed his eyes, unable to believe what he saw. Blood covered the floor and flowed through the tight channels between the stone blocks. The stench was harder to bear than the sight.

His knees wobbled, and he fell to the ground. He wiped his tears and crawled over to the first two bodies.

His mother and father. His mother's throat was slit clean. His father had received a knife to the heart and a single slash across the face.

The young man's tears splashed into his parents' blood. He lifted his gaze to the pile of bodies behind them. He recognized each and every face. The faces of his siblings. Six brothers and three sisters. They were all older and had helped raise him.

Now they were all dead. Just like *her*.

His father coughed up blood. The young man rushed to his side.

"Father!"

His father's eyes flickered. The young man wiped his father's mouth and face, but the deep gash stretched from his forehead to his chin. Regardless, he ripped his own shirt off and put pressure on the bleeding. The cloth was soon stained a dark red.

"Father?"

"Son…" His father's voice strained and cracked.

"Father! I'm here!"

"I am… sorry."

"It's okay, Father! It's okay!" He looked around the flaming cellar. The fire was still spreading. "We need to get you out of here!"

"I only wanted to push you," his father mumbled. "Youngest needs to be pushed. I was the youngest too."

"Father, we need to go!"

"No… I am gone… Save yourself. Save the family."

"Come on!" He tried lifting his father, but the weight was too much. He coughed on the smoke as he struggled and had to lay his father back down.

"Go, my son… I love you."

His father's eyes closed and his head fell to the stone ground.

"No!" he screamed. "Father? Father!"

The blaze burned through one of the barrels and released its contents. Red wine poured and splashed into the cellar and covered the floor. A second barrel ruptured and spilled more red wine. One after another, more barrels discharged their wine into the cellar.

The young man rose to his feet and waded through wine and blood despite the growing flames and thick smoke. He gazed upon a great wooden chest untouched by flame. He slid his fingers across the old oak. His fingers moved all the way down the smooth surface to the large lock.

A metal hoe rested against the wall near the chest. He grabbed it and banged it against the lock. Several knocks proved futile. The fire continued its relentless spread, and more and more wine gushed into the cellar.

The wine flowed knee deep, and he choked on the smoke, but the young man kept going. Kept thinking. He moved his attention to the wooden lid and bashed the tool into it. It weakened. He struck the lid again and again and soon pushed right through. He widened the hole with more strikes, but did so carefully. He reached his hand inside and pulled out its contents.

Rootstocks of his father's revered Cabernet Franc.

With a handful of rootstocks, he hurried out of the cellar door and out of the gagging smoke. He looked around and saw no one. The fires had spread throughout the entire valley and scorched the vineyards, leaving behind neat rows of charred vines.

He wiped the remaining tears from his face and coughed out the rest of the smoke. He took off his wine-soaked boots and looked over to his family's villa. It was engulfed in flames and collapsing one piece at a time.

He peered up to the ridge of the valley where he had spent time with his beloved earlier that morning. It still remained untouched by the fire and destruction and death. And with his father's rootstocks safely on his person, the young man climbed the valley slope to the ridgeline.

He looked back at the fiery valley where the morning sun shined bright. Most of the grapevines had burned down, and the villas too. Bodies lay scattered throughout the land. Most of the men dressed as knights had mounted and seemed ready to leave, job well done.

He remembered the young woman. He remembered his brothers and sisters. He remembered his mother. And he remembered his father.

He repeated in his head what his father told him. *Youngest needs to be pushed*.

The young man felt pushed.

Tread against wind and dried leaves
Crunching underneath boots in silence
Flesh remains separate and grieves
Stand and wait for the gentle sirens

Spoon Man

Spoon Man. Spoon Man. The words repeated in my head over and over. It had such a whimsical ring to it. The perfect name for such a mysterious man.

The stories from classmates offered pieces of the puzzle, glimpses of the story, but it was all hearsay. All of it except for one thing. The one thing that sprouted every rumor and every tale. Thousands of spoons decorated his lonely property in the nearby forest.

I write this story because I met Spoon Man one afternoon. An afternoon I will never forget, not in a hundred years. It was all because I wanted to win *Best Student Journalist* at my high school so I would be accepted by my dream college. And this was the story of all stories. Romantic, I know. I lost the award, but the visit remains close to me.

The overgrown foot trail to his home was a long and arduous one. Nearly two miles from the road but worth every step. The weather had cooled the previous week, and the leaves were beginning to change. Autumn rustled and blew, but when I arrived at the cabin, everything seemed still.

All but the wooden spoons.

The spoons hung in rows from the porch ceiling, along the roof and around the chimney, and they swung from the branches of trees. They knocked and clanked together with the shifting breeze, echoing in the empty woods. The entire property was adorned like a festival. But there was no sign of anyone or anything else. The unrehearsed symphony remained the only evidence of habitation.

The closer I walked, the more unmistakable the details of the spoons became. Carved from a variety of wood, they were stunning. Pristine and well-designed, sanded and oiled, some even painted with colors and patterns. Every shape and size you could imagine. The diligence and craftsmanship were obvious. Spoon Man had incredible talent. It must have been from all the practice.

And with each stride forward, my heart raced.

The rotted porch rose three steps, and each one creaked louder than the last. I avoided the protruding nails in the floorboards and arrived at the door. To the left was an empty rocking chair swaying in the same breeze the spoons danced with. Spoons even dangled overhead as I reached for the screen door. It hung on a single hinge, and the screen was so badly ripped its purpose was lost.

It screeched a deafening protest that caused me to hesitate. I took another breath and slipped my hand through and knocked three times. But not until the seventh set of knocks did someone answer.

My stomach sank through the porch as the door crept open. A long gray beard and wrinkled face greeted me. His eyes were heavy and his ears were big. His tattered clothes looked even older than he did.

"How many times do you plan to knock?" he asked in an aggravated yet fragile tone.

I tried to respond. I wanted to respond. But instead, my legs turned and dashed back the way I came. They ran me down the trail before my mind could catch up and stop.

I stared back down the footpath at Spoon Man's cabin. I tried to slow my thumping heart, but it was pointless. A droplet of water splashed onto my nose from the sky, and I looked up, only to be struck by another on my forehead. And then another. I ran back toward the cabin as fast as I could as the rain worsened.

It only got heavier, and it all happened so quick. I was soaked before I reached the cabin again. I collapsed onto the hardwood underneath the roof of the porch and enjoyed the dryness. The sound of the rain pinging on the tin roof nearly put me to sleep. It reminded me of my old house in my old town.

The clanking of wooden spoons pulled me away from further reminiscing. And when I looked up, the front door was wide open.

I wiped my boots on the old mat and stepped into the cabin. It was dimly lit, but well organized and clean. A single lantern illuminated the kitchen area, but most of the light came from a burning wood stove with an open hatch.

Two chairs faced the stove. One was occupied.

Unlike the porch, the wood floors on the inside made little to no sound. The heavy rain drilling the tin roof above faded into the background and gave room for two more noises: the carving of wood and the burning of wood.

I stepped with slow feet as burnt wood and tobacco filled my nostrils. Suddenly, he stopped carving and sat back in his chair. He placed the carving knife onto a small table beside him.

"The closer you are to the fire, the faster you'll dry." He picked up a smoking pipe next to the knife and puffed. He took a deep drag and held it tightly in his lungs. He blew out three rings that floated across the cabin in the light of the fire before fading away and disappearing.

"May I carve you a spoon?"

"Uh, yes," I replied. "Please."

The million questions I had prepared ran through my mind, but I had a few new ones as well. Why would he want to carve one for a total stranger? Why had he let me in and no one else? Have more made it inside? Does he carve spoons for everyone he kills? Is that why there are so many?

No one knows where I am.

I realized I was still standing in the middle of the floor. Spoon Man had put the pipe back down on the table and gone back to carving.

I decided to keep walking despite my instinct to run and never look back. I moved one foot in front of the other and approached the empty chair beside Spoon Man. The warmth from the fire was inviting and helped pull me in. I dragged my feet to the front of the chair and placed myself on its cushion.

My eyes lifted to the man's face, but he was

busy with his carving. He moved the blade along the grain and worked on the rough design of a project that clearly resembled a spoon. The careful stroke of a sharpened blade against green wood was crisp and satisfying to the ear. The way he manipulated the knife against the wood fascinated me and appeared so precise that you would not believe he was an old man.

"You must have come here for something." he asked, never breaking the stroke of his knife against the wood.

I fumbled the words in my head. While they bounced around chaotically, my tongue twisted into a thousand knots. I tried to swallow, but my mouth was a desert. Finally, a single word came free.

"You."

Spoon Man turned my way and smiled. And when he did, his teeth were not rotten and crooked like I expected. They were a sparkling white, even better than my own. I tried to relax in the chair, but I couldn't. I sat there as stiff and nervous as a student next in line to present a project he had not prepared.

"Where would you like to start?" He went back to carving. "It's been a long time. I could use the conversation." Shaping the bottom of the spoon bowl, he worked his way back and forth to create a smooth curve. I watched in awe before remembering I had a question to answer.

"Why?" I stuttered. That was all I had, and Spoon Man chuckled.

"Why *what*?" he asked.

"Why… spoons? And why me?" I forced

myself farther back into the chair.

"Spoons are practical and useful," he said matter-of-factly. "And no one's ever knocked before." He paused and held the spoon up to the light of the stove for a better look. He measured the edges with his eyes and must have noticed something, because he went straight back to carving.

"No one's knocked before? But all the stories…"

"You don't believe everything you hear, do you?" He held out the spoon for another inspection. "Especially from children."

"I'm not a child!" I insisted. "I'm seventeen."

"When you get to be my age, everyone under fifty is a child." Spoon Man rested the spoon on his lap and the knife on the table. He pressed the pipe against his lips again and lit a match. The tobacco leaves burned and filled the room with their scent. He took a large puff and blew two more smoke rings that traveled past me.

"Having thousands of spoons is not practical or useful," I said, or wished I said. What I did manage to spill was far less eloquent: "Why *all* the spoons?"

"Because I feel alive when I carve them. I feel *something*." Spoon Man's eyes pierced my own like a javelin. His gaze shifted back to his pipe as quickly as it arrived. He thumbed the tobacco and lit another match.

I think he wanted me to ask more. I think he needed me to. So I used my new favorite word.

"Why?"

He took another puff from his pipe and exhaled

the smoke. But this time no rings. He placed it back on the table and picked up a different knife, one with a hooked blade. The instrument was put to work carving out the inside of the spoon bowl.

"I'm Swedish," he offered. "Woodcarving is in my blood." A loud crack from the fire nearly launched me from my seat. I settled back into the cushion and saw that Spoon Man had stopped carving and was staring deep into the wood stove. "And because the love of my life died fifty-seven years ago. That's why there are so many. I've had fifty-seven years to do them all."

He went back to carving. I closed my mouth and scrambled for another question.

"But why spoons?" I asked. World-class journalist, I was.

"Because I was carving her a spoon." He paused his knife stroke but only briefly. He continued again, with more force than before. "I was carving her a spoon. She was a cook and specialized in soups. She used many spoons. And it was my first carved spoon. I had finally finished it and rushed to give it to her. But she was dead. Car accident... if you can call it that. Drunk driver striking a Swedish immigrant's Danish wife in 1947? Forget about justice. I burned the spoon in a fire and have never felt the same. The last time I can say I was happy was when I was carving a spoon. So here I am, two thousand, four hundred and seventy-two... three spoons later, but happiness still avoids me."

His voice cracked on the last word, and my heart stopped. But he kept carving the spoon, never once breaking concentration on the task. My heartbeat resumed, and I was able to relax in the chair again.

Spoon Man was no lunatic in the woods who shoved spoons down your throat and up your asshole until you agreed to pray to his spoons, as Tommy Fletcher and the others claimed. Instead, he was a heartbroken old man who had spent his life trying to recapture feelings of love.

"That's beautiful," I said. What else could I say? It *was* beautiful. Like a poem written centuries ago.

"No, it is not." Spoon Man stopped carving and looked at me. His eyes gazed upon mine so intently that I could see the pain in each and every year of those fifty-seven. He then stood from his chair and stepped into the kitchen, where he collected a couple of items.

I turned to watch but remained in my chair. He wetted a rag with grapeseed oil and rubbed the entire spoon methodically several times.

I searched for words, but my mind was useless. Silence prevailed.

Spoon Man studied his creation one last time. A smile sprung onto his face after checking all the angles, curves and sides. He walked back and held the spoon out to me. I accepted the gift and studied it myself.

The smooth design of the bowl and handle were magnificent. But he carved it so quickly and with such ease. A true master craftsman.

"It's gorgeous," I remarked, and he appeared glad for the compliment.

"Keep it outside in the moisture for a few weeks." He picked up his pipe and thumbed the tobacco. "The grapeseed oil will hasten the settling process, but it will still crack if it dries out too much."

Without another word, he strolled to the front door of the cabin. Sunshine poured onto his face, and he seemed to enjoy the warmth on his pale skin. I was so enthralled by the man himself, I had not even noticed the pinging on the tin roof had stopped. He stepped outside and left the door open like an invitation. Soon the rocking chair could be heard swinging back and forth.

I finally stood from the chair and joined him. A soft breeze greeted my cheeks, and the sun shined bright. The dark clouds had passed, and the day appeared heavenly once more. Rainwater dripped from the roof and the trees and splashed into puddles. Birds chirped and a squirrel chased another across a tree branch decorated with spoons.

The smell of the woods after a storm always soothed my senses. I could not help but smile.

He rocked in his chair and loaded more tobacco into his pipe. He puffed calmly on the fresh leaves. A train of smoke rings left his mouth and danced through the humid air before dissipating. He turned to me with a noticeable smile.

"*This* is beautiful."

My agreement was obvious and the two of us enjoyed the sounds and smells of the forest. The decorated parcel of land was absolutely delightful and would leave anyone in awe. When I first arrived, my initial impulse was fear. I had never been filled with such despair. But in hindsight... how foolish was I?

Spoon Man appeared to look upon me with more and more gratitude. The wrinkled bags under his eyes seemed less heavy when he gazed into mine.

"I think that's my last spoon," he said.

"What do you mean?"

"I'm retiring." He thumbed the tobacco. "Hanging up my knives, if you will." He finished the contents of the pipe with another puff.

"Why?" I found myself holding the spoon with even more care. It was special.

"I no longer wish to carve spoons. I found what I was seeking."

"Forks then?"

Spoon Man laughed. He had a great laugh, which made me laugh. We must have laughed for five minutes. And then I decided to leave. I wanted to stay but I felt like I should leave. I did not want to ruin our perfect afternoon by staying too long. So we said goodbye.

I found what I was seeking.

The words echoed in my head the entire hike back to my car. I had no idea what to make of the whole thing, to be honest. It was beautiful, it was bizarre. So unexpected. I was not even sure it happened. But then I felt the hardwood of the spoon in my hand and held it out for another look.

It *did* happen.

Darkness swallowed the town before I arrived back home. I was brief with my parents and skipped dinner, to their confusion. I only wanted to be upstairs at my desk with paper and pen.

So I did just that and got to work. I wrote all night. I wrote down everything. Every little detail I could remember. I wrote the last period just before three in the morning.

It was finished.

I had goosebumps and could not wait to publish it in the school's newspaper. But would anyone even believe me? I looked to my left and there it was. The only proof I had. Spoon Man's spoon.

Keep it outside in the moisture for a few weeks.

His soft voice rang through my head, so I leapt from my desk and stepped out onto the back deck. I placed the precious spoon to rest on the ledge of the deck railing. I stayed out there for a moment to appreciate its beauty in the moonlight.

I fell asleep despite my excitement and dreamed of spoons. Of Spoon Man. Of the entire afternoon.

But the next morning, the spoon was gone. I looked everywhere on the deck, under the deck, around the yard, but it had vanished. I cried for hours.

Three days later, I went back to the cabin, and all the spoons were gone. Not a trace or piece of evidence remained except for the cabin itself. And even that was empty and looked abandoned.

But the wood stove was still warm.

I went home, uncertain if any of it had even happened. Again. But had no spoon to remind me this time.

I cried more.

I never published the story and never spoke of

Spoon Man again. At least not for the last fourteen years. Not until this publication. And that was why I failed to win the Best Student Journalist award at school, but it never stopped me from going to my dream college.

Wet the stone and grip the handle
Grind the tired edge back and forth
Using the light of a single candle
Reunion in south but facing north

Seeking

The Black Forest darkened with each stride.

Bruxton and Drunn reckoned it was midday, but sunlight dared not pierce the thick canopy of gnarled trees and branches. Drunn remained close to the light of Bruxton's torch as his companion hacked at the thorn-covered vines.

The darkness outside the circle of torchlight was as scary as it was unknown. Drunn kept his head on a swivel. Every sound, crunch or rustle snatched his attention and held it. But only until the next.

The insects were loudest. Humming, buzzing, squirming, fluttering, slithering. All of it created a constant and uneasy tone surrounding them. The torch kept the critters at bay but would do little against a large predator.

The two men had no idea what they were seeking.

Broken fences, slain livestock and missing property offered only clues and nothing more. The most telling indication was always the great big tracks left behind in the mud, dirt, everywhere. The tracks had to belong to a massive beast. And it had to be living in the Black Forest.

The beast's presence had only been felt in the last year. Where did it come from? Perhaps it widened its hunting territory. Perhaps it lost its previous one to an even larger predator.

The questions remained unanswered because no one had seen or heard the beast despite its great size. No one except Hargerrard. He was the first *human* victim.

"May we stop a moment?" Drunn asked.

"No." Bruxton waved his torch at a giant winged insect as it frantically tried to escape the light. Slimy wings brushed against Drunn's nose in his attempt to dodge it. The ugly creature disappeared into the black of the forest.

"I would like to scribble some notes." Drunn wiped his face thoroughly.

"No."

"Tales are more powerful when you feel what the characters feel. I want to capture those feelings, Bruxton. My feelings. Your feelings. The darkness. The sounds. I want to capture it all."

"I am certain you will feel the same when we stop. I am also certain the darkness *and* the sounds will follow us wherever we go."

"But—"

"No."

So they trekked on.

The ominous sounds of the forest grew in both volume and number the deeper they traveled. Staring eyes seemed to watch their every move as the pair passed through. The torch burned low, and the brush thickened. Drunn's worry multiplied.

Thorns and spines decorated every plant and shrub. The sharp needles scraped and cut the pants and skin of both men as they trudged through, despite Bruxton's axe work. Blood sprinkled the greenery and appeared to attract creatures once the torchlight moved on.

Bruxton stopped and looked at his torch. It had burned so low it nearly scorched his hand. He held it to all sides of him and then above for a complete study of his surroundings. He tossed the torch into the center of a clearing and glanced back to Drunn.

"*Now* we stop."

Drunn dropped his satchel to the ground beside a tree. The weight off his shoulders was nice but not enough. He had to get off his feet too. They were killing him more than anything. He loosened his boots with relief.

He watched Bruxton in admiration. His companion cut down branches for firewood and added some to the torch, now a campfire.

Drunn moved his attention to his pack. He unbuckled the compartment and removed a leather-bound book, a bottle of ink and a quill.

"We will need to keep the fire going all night," Bruxton said.

"Is it night?" Drunn opened the book.

"It is night for us." Bruxton chopped down branches closer to Drunn, but he tried remaining focused on his book. He stopped at the first blank page and readied his quill.

"Do you think we will find it?"

"I think it will find us before we find it. This is its home."

"Comforting," Drunn said.

"If you wanted comfort, you should have stayed home."

"You insisted I come."

"I insisted someone who could write come." Bruxton cut down another branch even closer to a flinching Drunn. Wood chips flew, and some landed on him. Bruxton smiled. "You begged me to choose you."

"Oh, yeah? Well, I heard *you* could read and write. Why do you need anyone at all?"

Bruxton said nothing.

"It's because you know *I* am the best scribe in the village." Drunn wrote more notes. "And *you* the best warrior. *We* are the best men for the tasks at hand."

"I am not the best warrior."

"Then tell me who is better?"

"Many."

Drunn rested his quill on the page and studied him.

"You sell yourself short, Bruxton. For a small village, Goddard has produced many fine warriors over the ages. But none like you. And you, of all men, know that." Drunn paused. The sounds of the forest dominated until he continued. "Is it the word *warrior* that displeases you? Would you prefer *fighter*?"

Bruxton gazed over to his companion. "Do you wish me to leave you here?"

"No." Drunn picked up and dipped the quill. "But you would do well to remember my purpose. And also yours."

"My purpose is to rid the world of the beast."

"If that was your true purpose, you would not have invited me." Drunn wrote more notes before continuing. "Rid the world of the beast, yes, but we both know that is not all you seek."

There was a long pause.

"You seek redemption."

Bruxton swung the axe so hard it cut clean through the branch and into the forest floor. He ripped it from the ground, and insects crawled from the hole and scurried away from the light of the campfire.

"You seek redemption through a heroic act so that your name will live on forever," Drunn stated. "Or at least in a better light. And I seek to author a story that will allow *my* name to live on forever. We seek the same thing, Bruxton. And we need each other to do so. It's quite poetic if you ask me."

"I did not ask you." Bruxton tossed the rest of the firewood into a great pile. "Finish capturing your feelings and get some rest. We leave here when I say." He lay beside the fire with the axe in hand and closed his eyes.

"No dinner?" Drunn asked.

"No dinner."

"You don't even want to talk about the story?"

"Why would I want to do that?"

"It's *your* story, Bruxton. The one to save your family name. Important, no?"

Bruxton rolled over and turned his back to Drunn.

"Well," Drunn resumed, "It's important to me and I cannot decide what perspective to write from.

All the best tales are from the hero's perspective. It's the most effective for a story, right? You get to experience the story through the hero whom everyone adores. People want to know and feel what the hero knows and feels. But what if I wrote from the perspective of someone else? From the perspective of the hero's companion? A man who is more afraid and warier than the brave hero and *also* just as likable. Not much is written in that manner. Could be more interesting, no? Something to think about."

Bruxton pretended to snore. Drunn continued, "I'm writing the story from the companion's point of view, I think. From *my* point of view, of course. The loveable companion."

Drunn stayed up and filled more pages. He only stopped to throw more wood onto the fire when it sounded as if something big was moving near their camp. Was it the beast? Was the fire enough to keep whatever it was away?

He finally fell asleep.

"Wake up!" Bruxton knocked him in his ribs.

Drunn awoke in a painful flinch after little sleep. Bruxton held a new torch into the dying fire until it caught and then kicked dirt over the fire once the torch was ready.

Drunn rose to his feet, but slowly.

Bruxton stood with a new sense of urgency. A new sense of purpose. "Let's go."

"I changed my mind." Drunn rubbed his temple.

"Huh?"

"I changed my mind about the point of view.

It's traditionally written from the perspective of the hero because that's who the audience cares about. There must be a reason for that, and I should not mess with it if I expect to be remembered. It might be an easy way to be forgotten."

Bruxton shook his head and walked away with the torch. Drunn quickly gathered his satchel and tossed it around his shoulder.

"That's an important development." Drunn rushed up to Bruxton to stay in the safety of the flame. "That means I'm going to need more of your inner thoughts and feelings to capture the true essence of the story."

Bruxton chuckled. "So now you want to capture *my* feelings?"

"Yes. To write the story *you* are depending on."

And they trekked on.

They walked for what seemed like a full day, but Bruxton had given up on trying to keep track of time long ago. It was hopeless. Morning, midday, night. It was all the same. He was not even certain they stopped at night or started in the morning, but none of that mattered. There was only one time of day in this forest, and that was night. So they traveled through the night.

"You plan to die killing the beast, don't you?" Drunn suddenly asked.

Bruxton walked on.

"That's why I'm here, is it not? To record what happens because you will not be returning to the village to tell it yourself."

Bruxton walked on.

"I will write whatever I damn well please if you

do not talk to me."

Bruxton stopped. He snapped his gaze back to Drunn and studied the small man. Drunn had called his card. His presence was critical for that exact reason. He had chosen Drunn because he was skilled and young and ambitious.

"Yes," Bruxton finally said. "What I have done will never be forgiven while I am still breathing. The only chance for my sons and daughters, and their sons and daughters, will be if I sacrifice my life for the good of the people. For the good of *everyone*. Only in my death will my family be able to live."

Drunn looked stunned and for once had nothing to say. Bruxton rather liked it. Maybe if he answered more of his questions, he would shut up. That would be nice.

"I hope you will not include such information in your tale," Bruxton said. "Such things would only tarnish my actions and sink my name deeper into the dirt. For my family, tell the story that truly matters. You will receive what you wish all the same. Do I have your word that this remains between us?"

The response was slow. The sounds of the Black Forest dominated the moment. Some fluttering, some slithering. A loud buzzing passed nearby. Drunn responded just before his companion's patience ran out.

"Yes, yes. You have my word."

So they trekked on.

Bruxton hacked away at the gnarled growth while Drunn nibbled on a piece of dry bread. He finished the last of his canteen, savoring the last few drops on his tongue.

"I am out of water," Drunn confessed.

"You should have brought more."

"Do you think we will come upon some?"

No answer.

"A river? A stream?" Drunn continued. "I mean, it must rain in here a great deal for all this growth. But it makes you wonder… how does it all grow without sunlight? Does this place ever get sunlight?"

Bruxton stopped, and Drunn bumped into him because he was following too close. He lowered the torch and moved it along the ground.

"What is it?" Drunn gazed over Bruxton's shoulder. "Are those tracks?"

"Same ones from the village." Bruxton stared in the direction the tracks headed. He stared as if he could see something, but there was only darkness. He looked back to the tracks for further study. They were huge. Larger than he remembered from the village but no doubt the same. The base of the print was circular, with four protruding claws that dug deep into the dirt as the beast pushed off. Broken twigs and branches from the thorned brush confirmed the direction the beast took. Drunn looked scared.

"Come on." Bruxton followed the tracks. "You can capture your feelings later."

So they trekked on.

The sounds of the forest persisted as the two tracked the beast. A more defined trail appeared over time. It was used by more than just the beast.

Tracks of all kinds were imprinted along the way.

The beast had the largest prints, but it was another that captured their attention. It was most peculiar. Bruxton shined the torch across the ground.

The print of a man's boot.

He looked back to Drunn with a curious glance.

"Is that what I think it is?" Drunn swallowed.

Bruxton moved along the trail with the torch.

"Are we backtracking?" Drunn asked. "Is the beast following us?"

"We are not backtracking," Bruxton insisted.

"Where did the beast's prints go?" Drunn asked.

"Good question." Bruxton backtracked, careful to leave all the prints uncompromised. Drunn studied them too. They walked to the area where the beast's tracks vanished.

"No sign of it leaving the trail." Bruxton said. "They just… disappear."

"And the boots begin," Drunn added.

The two men looked to one another with astonishment, confusion and everything in between. They gazed back down at the tracks, hoping to make sense of it all, but their efforts were unrewarded. Drunn grabbed his satchel and unbuckled the main compartment.

"It's clear what we do," Bruxton said. "We follow the human tracks."

"Can I have a few moments?"

"No."

"Please?"

"We keep moving." Bruxton did not want to

answer questions anymore. He had too much on his mind. Could it be true? Humans?

So they trekked on.

The boot prints led them down the trail to a small encampment. Bruxton stopped and signaled Drunn to do the same. He crouched and lowered the light behind some brush. No one seemed to notice their arrival despite the glowing of the torch. No one even seemed to be home either unless they were in the three tents. A well-used fire pit with plenty of firewood sat at the center, and a pile of tools stacked in no particular order stood to one side.

Bruxton poured the remainder of his water onto the torch.

"Oh, come on!" Drunn complained.

Bruxton snuffed the torch into the ground until it was out. Darkness enveloped the area, and the encampment disappeared in the black. The sounds of the forest became even more haunting without the torch.

"What are you doing?" Drunn whispered.

"They will see the light."

"Who?"

"Whoever calls this home."

"But now we cannot even see ourselves!"

"Your eyes will adjust. Patience."

"Patience? What if no one lives here anymore? Who in their right mind would do so to begin with?"

"People still live here. You saw the tracks. They are not old. Look at the fire pit. Please tell me you are not so naive."

Bruxton and Drunn remained silent while they

waited. They waited for their eyes to adjust and for people to return. The latter would take much longer.

"What exactly is our plan?" Drunn swatted a juicy insect. "You know, when… if anyone shows up?"

"We get answers."

"Answers?"

"Yes. Answers."

"Answers to what?" Drunn frantically cleared his boots of something trying to crawl inside. "Why anyone would live out here? I would love to hear the answer to that."

Bruxton shot him a glance.

"There are several tents," Drunn continued. "What if there's a whole group of them? What are we going to do? Your destiny might involve death but mine does not. I understand death ensures a notable life for you. But life ensures a notable death for me."

A pause. Slithering, humming, wriggling.

"And on the subject," Drunn said. "I was thinking. Perhaps choosing a point of view is obsolete. Perhaps the most effective story is to understand all points of view. To see through the eyes of every character. To be an omnipotent narrator and offer the insights and feelings of all characters all the time. To tell a tale from the eyes of God. What do you think, Bruxton?"

"You will be God?"

"Yes, I suppose."

"I think you should stay here when the men come back."

"Do you think the story will be too muddied

with all that going on? Too complicated to follow?" Drunn's mind raced around and around. He had the perfect story but had no idea how to tell it. His options were endless. They always were for any tale. So many aspects, so many elements, so many ways to align each piece, but only one was best.

"It will be easier for me to take them on by myself." Bruxton ignored him. "Men are easier to kill than an unknown beast. They are predictable and full of fear." Second thoughts crept into Bruxton's head. Second thoughts about bringing anyone, especially a writer. Never invite a writer into your home, his trainer once warned. Maybe he should have done this alone. He would never have returned, his death would be assumed, but the beast would stop coming to the village. His success would be assumed as well. But he did not want them to assume.

He needed them to *know*.

"Wait, what? Kill?" Drunn shivered at the idea.

"These men *are* the beast."

"Then we should bring them back to face the court for their wrongdoing," Drunn insisted. "Not *kill* them."

Bruxton laughed. "Life is not like it is in your books, Drunn. In life, justice is best served by the sharp end of a sword, or axe. No one's time is wasted and no guilty man goes free. But you should write of a beast. You should write of a great beast and a great battle with it."

"Why?"

"No one will want to know the beast was man. It would only add to the mistrust among folk in town and perhaps even spark similar ideas for others. No good would come from it. And it would make for a better tale, no?"

"Hide the lie between two truths…" Drunn said as if quoting an old mentor. "Maybe it *should* be written from your point of view."

Bruxton held up one hand to silence any further words. A small glow from down the path approached at a steady pace. He watched and carefully lowered his hands to the grips of his sheathed sword and axe. The glow divided into three torches carried by three men.

The men had chunks of raw meat and a few tools. They were terribly unshaven and unkempt. One of them wore giant boots. The other two had similar boots slung over their shoulders, but walked in normal ones. They appeared tired and dragged themselves into camp.

They tossed their torches into the fire pit, where some brush and a few uncharred logs caught ablaze.

The man untied his strange boots as soon as he sat down beside the fire. He removed them from his feet with a sigh. "These things seem to get heavier and heavier every time," the man said, tossing them near a tent.

"That's why we always bring another pair of boots," another said as he hung raw meat over a rope above the fire pit. The tools were added to the pile of others. "Why all of a sudden you insist on wearing them all the way back to camp is beyond me."

"Because of my dream."

"Oh, here we go again. You've been paranoid

ever since that damn dream."

"No one is venturing in here, sonny. You know that."

"How long are we going to keep doing this?"

"Until we have enough tools to sell. You know that as well."

"What's the rush anyway? I've grown a taste for this life."

"It's not the worst I've done."

"Need to get laid though."

"Ay. Next time, we grab a broad and take turns."

The three men laughed.

"She wouldn't dare flee into the forest alone. She'll be a prisoner without bars."

They laughed harder.

"I say we go back for her tomorrow. Pick the ripest one of the lot."

"We have never gone two days in a row."

"How do you even keep track of days in here?"

"I have told you how many times? If you do not understand by now, you never will."

Drunn tapped Bruxton on the shoulder and startled him. The retired warrior had been watching with both curiosity and disgust. He spat on the ground.

"What's the plan?" Drunn whispered.

Bruxton turned and signaled for him to stay like a dog. He rose to his feet and drew his sword. He held the axe in the other hand.

He must have made a sound, because all three men snapped their necks to look in his direction. They stared right at him. But saw nothing but black.

"Like I'm the only one paranoid?" The man roared with laughter, and another joined him.

"Build up the fire," one said sternly, but the others couldn't hear through the laughter. "Build up the fire!" he yelled, and the others quickly did as they were told.

"So you did hear something?"

"Nothing the fire won't keep away."

Bruxton waited with a watchful eye. These men sickened him to the pit of his stomach. He gripped the sword and axe tighter. He thirsted for blood. He thirsted for blood like he had when he was a young warrior. He wanted three more heads for his collection.

"What if someone did follow us?"

"No one followed us!"

Bruxton stepped forward. The crunch of twigs and brush grabbed all three men's attention again, but Bruxton cared little. He kept going. His pace hastened to a charge.

This was it. This was his death and rebirth.

All three drew swords and pointed them at the darkness. Bruxton entered the light of the fire and swung his sword at one of them. The man blocked it, but the axe came too quickly and sliced deep into his shoulder. Blood squirted high and far and decorated the tents on his way to the hard ground.

Bruxton looked at the other two men. He stretched his neck for a moment and then charged.

But a loud scream interrupted. Drunn yelled in the distance and scurried about. A nightmarish bug must have crawled on him.

Bruxton resumed his charge.

This time, he swung the axe first. He swung it so hard he knocked his opponent to the ground. Bruxton swung again with the axe but again it was blocked, and the man did well to regain his feet.

Bruxton looked around for the third man.

He was gone.

"It's *you*," the man in front of him said.

Bruxton focused back on his opponent. He attacked him with the sword, then the axe and then the sword again. Two blocked strikes, but the third ruptured the back of his knee. He went down and spilled copious amounts of blood. He swung recklessly and with little hope, and Bruxton evaded with ease.

He sliced the man's sword-wielding hand clean off to add to the spray of blood on the tents. The man begged him as Bruxton placed the tip of his sword against the center of the man's throat and pushed in.

The man choked on his own blood. Bruxton watched him die and enjoyed it. The world would be a better place. The beast was dead. Or nearly dead. One left.

Bruxton looked for signs of the third man, and he quickly found him. He was escorting Drunn into the light of the fire with a dagger across his throat.

"I'm so sorry, Bruxton," Drunn admitted.

Bruxton dropped the axe and sword and displayed his empty hands. "I have nothing else. I promise this."

"I don't believe you!" the man yelled.

"Let him go and you will live," Bruxton replied.

"I don't believe anything you say! I know who you are!"

Bruxton closed his eyes. He had lived with the weight of his reputation for far too long. "That is no longer who I am." He unbuttoned his shirt. "Let him go and you will live. I promise this."

He slipped the sleeves from his arms and dropped the shirt onto the ground. Nothing but skin to see. And scars. Many scars.

"What are you doing?" the man yelled. "What the hell is this?"

"He's telling the truth!" Drunn insisted with watery eyes. "Please! Please, do not kill me. No one else needs to die! Not you, not me, not him."

"Shut up!" The man pressed the blade closer against his throat, and a small bead of blood dribbled down his neck and shirt.

Bruxton untied his boots and slipped them off.

"I ain't falling for your tricks, murderer!"

Bruxton untied his drawstring and pulled down his trousers. There he stood, clad only in white underwear that reached his knees. His chest, arms, legs, his entire body was littered with cuts and scars of old, but no weapons.

"I hide nothing. I have no weapons and no tricks. I promise this." He closed his eyes once more and took another deep breath. "Kill me instead."

"Kill you instead?" The man laughed. "How about I kill both of you!"

He sliced Drunn's throat and threw the dagger.

Bruxton moved his head and dodged the blade. His companion collapsed to the ground in slow motion. It seemed to take an eternity for him to land in the pool of his own flowing blood.

The man looked at Bruxton with surprise and fear. He turned and fled the light of the fire without hesitation and never looked back.

Bruxton grabbed his axe from the ground and closed his eyes. He listened carefully to the trampling and rustling of brush as the man blindly ran through the darkness. His eyes remained shut as he aimed the axe and threw it with complete focus.

The sound of an axe striking the spine of a screaming man told him everything he needed to know.

He opened his eyes and knelt down beside Drunn. He was already dead.

Bruxton stared at the fire and lost himself in it for what seemed like days, weeks. Only when the flame began to die did he come to. He added another two logs and then remembered Drunn's book.

He walked into the darkness where they had waited for the men to return. He found Drunn's satchel and dusted off the bugs. He brought it over to the fire and took out the book. He opened it and read.

He read each page and every word. Flashes of smiles appeared on his face but were dismissed as fast as they came. When he finished the written pages, tears rolled down his cheeks. He wiped his face clean and then ripped the pages out. He tossed them into the fire and watched them burn. He watched them burn like he had watched that man die.

Pieces of burning paper danced in the air above.

He reached back into the bag and removed the ink and quill. He was not much of a scribe. He only learned to read after the papers praised him as one of the best warriors in the land. And he only learned to write when those same papers trashed his reputation and family name.

"This time, my friend, we will hide the truth between two lies." He dipped the quill into the ink three times and wrote on the page.

Drunn The Beast Slayer

Witness glories fall and never rise
How the cold bites deep and numbs
Far beyond the screams and the cries
Listen with care for unending drums

The Cost of Three

THE JOB

His heart pounded like a ceremonial drum before a sacrifice. Morning sunlight poured onto the new paint of Mark Frasier's luxury car. Sweat dripped from his nose, and his hands shook nervously.

He drove into the empty parking lot of a corporate building and backed into a space next to the bay doors for loading and unloading trucks. He straightened out twice and checked his gold watch. 6:42 am.

He closed his eyes and waited a moment. Today was the first day of his new life. He was still not sure what kind of life, but it would certainly not be a good one, not how he imagined it.

He opened his cell phone.

No missed calls and no missed texts.

Communication from his family would have done him wonders, but he clipped a security badge to his belt and exited the car. He did not lock it because he planned to be back soon, and in a hurry.

Mark wore no jacket, but the weather deserved one. Goosebumps ran down his arms as he trekked all the way to the front of the building, where double doors greeted him.

He swiped the badge and stepped inside.

Two security guards sat in chairs beside a metal detector and watched him enter, but not suspiciously. They nodded.

"You're early, Mark," Curtis said.

"Lots to do." Mark forced a smile.

"Don't you dare tell me the score," Eddie said. "I recorded it at home. Plan to fall asleep to it in a couple hours."

"I won't." Mark stepped through the metal detector.

No beep.

"Enjoy the day," Eddie said.

"You too." Mark continued through the building to where a series of elevators lined the hallway. He pressed the down button and waited. And waited. He stood there for an eternity. He peered over to the guards and back to the elevator, then back to the guards. They paid him no mind, but that did nothing to settle his heart rate. His sweat dripped onto the beautiful granite floor.

DING.

The elevator doors slid open and Mark stepped inside. He pressed the button labeled *B4* and then the one to close the doors. He pressed the latter again. And again.

The doors closed and the elevator descended.

Mark stared at his reflection in the stainless-steel interior. He studied the look on his face and the clothes on his back. This was it. Nothing would be the same.

The elevator traveled several stories and stopped at its destination. The door opened to reveal a metallic hallway. Two closed doors faced opposite one another and nothing else. He walked into the one labeled *MEN*.

He approached one of ten lockers and scrolled the combination lock. 32-17-28. He undressed and slipped into blue scrubs. He clipped the security badge to the waistband of the drawstring pants and checked his cell phone once more. 6:54 am and still nothing.

He tried centering his thoughts, but his conscience screamed over everything. It was impossible to think. He placed his phone and keys in his pocket.

The door swung open. Henry Goodison walked in and looked at Mark as if he had seen a ghost.

"Whoa, Mark." Henry approached his locker. "You startled me. Didn't expect to see anyone in this early."

"I have to catch up on a few things." Mark shut his locker. "You?"

"Uh, yeah. Me too. Did you have to work on Saturday?"

"Can't remember the last Saturday I didn't work. Where were you?"

"I asked for it off because it was my daughter's birthday." Henry smiled. "And they gave it to me, can you believe it?"

Mark smiled back. "Glad to hear it."

"And how about that game last night?"

"Missed it."

"You? Missed the game? Never thought I'd see the day."

"Who won?"

"Oh, I didn't see it either."

"See ya in there, Henry."

"Uh, wait, Mark?" Henry stood there in his boxer briefs as Mark turned. His eyes were troubled, and his mouth quivered as if ready to spill words, but his tongue refused to cooperate. "Never mind."

"Have a good day, Henry." Mark exited the other side of the bathroom. Another door requiring another badge swipe, and it led to a long corridor with bright fluorescent lighting.

He considered whether or not Henry had acted strangely. Whether he acted strangely. But he chalked it up to his imagination and shrugged it off.

He had bigger matters at hand.

Mark stopped at a sliding glass door. *B402.* He pressed a red button and the door opened. The room was small and had little except for dispensers of hairnets, beard nets, safety glasses, face masks, gloves, shoe covers, hand sanitizer, and alcohol wipes.

He gowned up and looked at the mirror on the wall. He always thought he looked silly in a hairnet, especially a beard net, but nothing seemed funny now. He stared deep into his own eyes. He wanted to cry but held it together.

"You can do this. For them."

He opened the sliding door into the next room and stepped inside. A short hall led to a single door with a digital clock overhead. 7:01 am. He swiped his badge once more and the door opened. Another airlock with additional gear. Three hazmat suits, large boots and thick gloves hung from hooks on the wall.

He put on the gear and stared at his reflection again. He barely recognized his own face, his own eyes. He punched the mirror to erase the stranger, and it shattered. Pieces rained down on the floor. Hundreds, maybe even thousands of pieces, in a Hygiene Zone Three airlock. A bizarre smile covered his face, but it was brief.

He turned to the next door. *B417.* He entered a seven-digit code into a keypad, and the automatic doors opened.

Three four-hundred-gallon stainless-steel kettles sat bolted to the floor. Tags on all three read *SULFURIC NINE.* A mutation of sulfuric acid that the company had patented four years earlier. A considerably more dangerous chemical than its parent.

Mark stared at the kettles before heading toward another door. He opened it to find a room loaded with fifty-gallon drums with toxicity warnings and special lids. Stacks of small platforms on wheels with the capacity to hold a barrel each lined the storage room as well. He unstacked and laid them out on the floor. He then worked to lift as many empty barrels as there were platforms.

He wheeled eighteen over to the kettles.

He attached a thick hose to the bottom of the first kettle. He secured the connection many times over and made several adjustments. He attached the hose to an engine pump and another to deliver product from the pump to the seal on top of the barrel lids. He inspected the connections, screws and seals a few more times.

When he was comfortable and after a deep breath, he released the lever underneath the kettle to allow Sulfuric Nine to flow freely into the hose, but not through the pump.

Mark looked at the clock on the wall. 7:18 am.

Plenty of time.

He pressed a couple of buttons on the engine pump screen, and it turned on. The hose vibrated as the chemical rushed into the barrel. The potent smell of the chemical stung his nostrils through the suit.

After thirty seconds, the pump clicked off. The barrel was full. Mark detached the hose and locked the seal on the lid, careful to hold the open end of the hose upward to avoid drips. He moved it to the next barrel and filled that one too. He did it over and over until all eighteen were full. He drained the first two kettles but only needed a hundred gallons from the third.

Nine hundred gallons of Sulfuric Nine.

It scared him to death.

7:41 am. Mark wheeled the barrels into another airlock after entering a code with his large gloved fingers. The airlock led to an open room with a sliding metal door. He fit as many barrels as he could and opened the other side. He moved the barrels in and then headed back for more. He managed it in four trips.

With all eighteen inside, he slipped out of the boots and hazmat suit. Back in his scrubs, he punched the code into the keypad beside the metal door, and it slid open.

It was an elevator.

He wheeled eleven barrels inside and clicked the button for the warehouse.

The elevator rose four stories while Mark watched the clock above the door. 7:49 am. The doors opened to reveal another airlock. He pushed the barrels inside and then into the large warehouse filled with rows and rows of pallet racks and materials. He unloaded the barrels from the elevator and headed back down for the others.

The warehouse clock read 7:54 am when he wheeled all eighteen to the third bay door. It took him nine trips. But on the seventh, he heard an elevator open farther down the warehouse.

He froze and waited.

Henry exited with a similar barrel on a platform. *HYDROCHLORIC FIVE.* The two found each other's eyes and hesitated. But they both knew. They knew they'd had comparable nights and were in the same position. Henry had a family, same as Mark. After the brief moment, the two men went back to work.

Mark opened the bay door.

A tractor trailer was parked against the door with its back already open. Two rugged men armed with scars and semi-automatic rifles waited with wry smiles.

One looked at his watch and used his rifle to signal Mark to work, so the helpless chemist sprang to action and pushed the barrels inside the trailer by himself.

The armed men watched and chuckled.

When he was done, one of the men waved his rifle toward Henry, so Mark helped his coworker wheel the Hydrochloric Five into the trailer as well.

"How's your family?" Mark whispered.

"I don't know. Yours?"

"I don't know."

The armed men closed the trailer door, and the truck drove away as if headed to a routine delivery. There was a sense of relief, but it was short-lived.

Mark and Henry found each other's eyes one last time and jumped out of the bay door without another thought. And despite their clumsy landings, they sprinted to their cars like Olympic athletes.

Mark fumbled his keys but recovered, rattling through them to find the one he needed. He found it and slammed it into the ignition. 8:06 am.

THE FAMILY

8:34 am. Mark had been gripping the steering wheel tightly for twenty-eight minutes. Each finger was sore, but he cared little. He only cared about the red light screaming in front of his car. It was an intense red that tortured all of his senses. He would have blown through it long ago. That would be an easy decision. But there was another vehicle stopped at the intersection.

A police cruiser.

Mark breathed heavily as the two cars waited at opposite ends of the red. He was convinced the officer was staring him down, as if he knew what he had just done.

The light flashed green, and Mark was off. The cruiser drove past without a second thought, but soon Mark was stuck behind a slow truck.

"Come on, come on, come on." He scanned the lane in front of the truck, but it was difficult to see if he could pass. He cut into the opposite lane, but an oncoming car came straight into view. He swerved back and regained control of the vehicle.

He sighed and remained behind the slow truck.

He looked at his cell phone again. Still nothing.

He called the house line, but it was disconnected. He tried his wife's cell phone, but it went straight to voicemail. He tried his son's cell phone. Same story. He took another deep breath and wiped his forehead.

Mark took a hard turn onto a street. He raced to the end and took another.

He skidded into the driveway of a massive home and leaped out of the car. He rushed through the lush garden entrance and toward the grand door. It was unlocked and partially open.

"Claire!" he yelled.

"Yes!" Her familiar voice floated from the other room. "Mark! Over here!"

He flew into the living room, and Claire surprised him with the biggest hug she had ever given him. It was more than a hug, squeezing tighter and tighter, like it would be the last. An embrace filled with every emotion possible.

"Daddy!" Kelsey joined in, and so did James. They all held one another and cried for what could never be enough time. Mark never wanted to leave.

"I love you so much." Mark wiped Claire's tears and then his own. They held the children tighter. He found his wife's eyes and swallowed. "Are they gone?"

"I think so," Claire replied.

"When did they leave?"

"Half an hour ago?" She looked to her children for confirmation.

James nodded. "Who were those guys, Dad?"

"They were bad men, James," Mark said.

"Bad men? That's it? I'm seventeen." He

stepped away from the family hug. "You helped them make a bomb, didn't you? A big one, right?"

"No, James, we don't know that for sure."

"Everyone knows you guys make all kinds of crazy shit down there. It's been all over the internet for years."

"Language…" Claire said.

"Language? I just had a gun to my head and I can't swear? Perhaps the *bad* men just plan to sell it for charity?"

"James…" Claire said, but Mark stayed quiet. He knew James was right.

His son stormed away from the living room and up the stairs. He stopped halfway and turned back to the family. "When do you think they find the time to polish their M16s with all that volunteer work?"

"They were going to kill us!" Mark shouted, but James slammed his bedroom door and said nothing more.

"Let him be." Claire pulled Mark back into her arms with Kelsey. She was still crying hard. "It's been a tough morning for all of us. Let's just call the police. They will know what to do next."

"The police?" Mark asked, surprised. "Do you remember what they said?"

"It's the *police*, Mark. They will protect us."

"These were no amateurs, Claire. I think we need to take their word."

"We have to go to the police, Mark. What else are we going to do?"

"What about Max?" Kelsey asked between sniffles. Mark looked to Claire.

"They said if we moved from the couch before

you came home they would know and it wouldn't be wise," Claire said.

"So you believed that?" Mark moved away. "What about everything else they said?"

He stepped closer to the kitchen door. He knew what he was going to find, but he wished it were different. He peered around the corner, and there he was. A Golden Retriever lying in a pool of blood. A resurgence of sadness took over his body and nearly dropped him to his knees.

MAX, the tag read. His eyes were open but lifeless. Mark stared deep into the pupils of the canine until Claire snapped him out of it.

"I told you I didn't like that job," she said.

"You only expressed concern before the money started flowing in."

She lowered her head in shame. "We should bury him."

"We don't have time."

"What do you mean?"

"We need to leave."

"Leave?"

"Yes, Claire." Mark held her hands. "The police will be here soon."

"Then we will talk to them, Mark."

"I think it's best we leave town. And now."

"Leave town?"

"The country."

"What do you mean? Where are we going?"

"Canada."

"Canada?"

"Yes, Canada. It's a seven-hour drive." Mark looked at the kitchen clock. 8:51 am. "Pack only what we need and what we can fit in the car."

"And then what? What the hell are we going to do in Canada? Live in hiding for the rest of our lives? What about the kids? What about school? The police will understand our situation, Mark. They had guns to our heads. You had no choice!"

"But what if something happens?"

"What do you mean?"

"What if James is right? What if they are making a bomb? People will demand justice. It will be hard living in this country once my role is exposed. Even if there's no prison time, we will still be a target. I think Canada is our best option right now. I don't know why, I just do. My gut tells me. Did you forget how specific those men were? What they would do to us if we contacted the police?"

Claire looked down at Max. "We should bury him first. For the kids."

"You and the kids pack. I'll dig a hole. We'll say a few words and then we're gone."

RING.

Mark and Claire jumped.

RING.

The telephone rang a second time, and they could only stare at it. After several more rings, the answering machine picked up.

"Hello." Mark's recorded voice played. "You have reached the Frasier residence. We cannot come to the phone right now, but if you leave your name, number and a brief message, we will get back to you as soon as possible. Have a great day."

BEEP.

"Hello, dear, it's your mother," a crackly voice

said. "There's this Wanted Man on the television that looks just like Mark. It reminded me to call you about that recipe you asked for. Banana pudding, right?"

Mark and Claire shared a glance. Ingredients and techniques from the speaker blended into the background of Mark's thoughts. He knew he would have no time to dig a hole. It ripped him to shreds, but Max would have to remain on the kitchen floor in his own blood. They needed to move and move quickly.

"Alright!" the phone speaker continued. "I hope to hear from you real soon and can't wait to see you in three weeks. Buh-bye!"

SIRENS. Distant but getting closer.

"Get the kids. Now!" Mark rushed into the four-car garage, where more luxury cars were parked. He opened a drawer in the custom workbench. A safe rested inside, and he turned the combination. 32-17-28. Same as work.

One 9mm Glock 19 and a full box of bullets.

He checked the full clip in the handle and emptied the box of bullets into his pocket. A few dropped onto the concrete floor as he tucked the handgun into his waistband and hid it under his shirt.

"This is the police!" a megaphone shouted.

The rest of the family rushed downstairs and headed to the back door.

"Come on, come on!" Mark grabbed his jacket.

"Step out of the house with your hands up!" the megaphone continued.

Mark led them into the backyard and ran. They

did not think. They just ran. They ran as fast and as far away from the house as they could.

The man with the megaphone spewed more orders, but the words faded.

The grassy backyard merged with the woods, and the Frasiers were into the tree line. Mark stopped for a glance back. Law enforcement flanked the house at several points and infiltrated with ease. Officers stormed the doors with guns aimed.

Mark caught up with his family.

THE DRIVER

The Frasiers scurried down a slope toward a road. Leaves covered the ground and made the terrain slippery. The descent grew steeper and did nothing to help.

Kelsey fell and tumbled down the hill. A car sped around the corner in the same direction.

Marked jumped and slid down the slope after her. He gained speed but was never going to catch her. He saw the car approaching, and the trajectory seemed disastrous. He could only be a spectator.

Kelsey rolled onto the pavement as the driver slammed on the brakes. The car swerved until the front bumper stopped inches from Kelsey's nose.

Mark scooped her away and apologized to the driver with his hand.

He stepped out of the car anyway. "Oh my God! I am so sorry! I didn't see you! Are you okay? I am so sorry. Oh my God. Are you hurt? Holy cow!"

"We're okay," Mark said. "We're okay. Thank you."

Claire and James finished their descent and joined them. Claire wrapped her arms around her daughter and landed kiss after kiss.

"Sweetheart! You're okay!"

"I am so glad to hear that," the driver said. "If there's anything I can do… Anything."

Mark looked to Claire, then back to the driver. "Can you give us a lift?"

"Uh, yeah, sure. Where are ya headed?"

"Just back to the trailhead. We got a little lost."

"Trailhead? I didn't even know there was a trail around here."

"Oh yeah… Silverback."

"Silverback?"

Mark nodded. "Silverback Trail. It's just down there."

"Well, alright then, get in. Name's Paul."

"Mar— Matt. This is my wife, Karen. My two children, Krystal and Jason."

"Nice to meet you all. And sorry again."

The rest of the family filled the back seats while Mark sat in the front with their new friend. Mark pulled out his phone and checked the time. 9:22 am. He slid the battery out and dropped them out the window.

Paul drove off and turned up the radio. "Did you hear about this?"

"There is still no sign of the Sulfuric Nine or Hydrochloric Five," the reporter announced, "but we can confirm the deaths of Henry Goodison, his wife and four children."

Mark shook his head.

Paul spoke over the reporter. "Thousands of gallons of this stuff was stolen from this fancy lab not too far from here. Enough to make tons of explosives, they say. Bombs to take out entire cities. And two scientists were behind it all. One of them just died, but the other is still on the run."

Paul turned up the volume.

"Mark Frasier is armed and dangerous. If you see him, please call the police. He is average height, has black hair and will probably be traveling with his family. A wife, a teenage son and a younger daughter. If you see them, please alert the authorities immediately!"

Paul gazed into the rearview mirror at the family. He looked at Mark, who smiled back nervously.

"I repeat," the reporter continued, "do not approach the family. Mark Frasier is armed and dangerous. Get to a safe place and call the police!"

Paul slammed on the brakes, but Mark drew his pistol and aimed. Claire gasped in surprise while Kelsey began crying again.

"Keep driving," Mark demanded.

Paul stared down the barrel and then into Mark's eyes. "Why?"

"We're innocent!" Claire pleaded.

"We had guns to our heads." Mark looked at his own gun. "Just as you do. Now drive."

"No."

Mark cocked the hammer of the Glock. "I said *drive*."

"If you're so innocent, why don't you go to the police?" Paul kept his foot firmly on the brake.

"It's not that simple."

"Neither is driving with a Wanted Man."

Mark aimed the pistol away from Paul's head

and squeezed the trigger.

BANG.

The recoil was harsh, and the sound filled the car. The driver's-side window shattered into pieces.

Kelsey screamed and cried harder. James shouted at his father and tried comforting her.

Claire was stunned and said nothing.

"Drive," Mark repeated.

Paul took a deep breath and slowly shifted his foot from the brake to the gas. He gazed out the windshield and crept back up to the speed limit without another word.

"Give me your cell phone," Mark demanded, so Paul did just that. "You're driving us to Canada."

THE SWITCH

10:15 am. The radio was off, and they had been driving for an hour. No one said a word. Mark had lowered his pistol but kept it in hand, ready.

"I'm a jazz guy," Mark said.

"What?" Paul asked.

"I'm a jazz guy. Blues, funk, rock." Mark turned on the radio and searched for a station. "What about you?"

"Screw you."

"You don't have to make this harder than it needs to be."

"You said *you* had guns to your heads, right?"

"Yes."

"And did you have small talk with the men aiming?"

"No."

"Well, then."

Mark aimed the pistol again. "What music do you listen to?"

Paul sighed. "Country."

Mark found a channel, and a speedy banjo solo rang through the car.

"Sorry about the gun," Mark admitted.

Paul chuckled sarcastically. "I'm sure you are."

Mark bobbed his head to the tune, but Paul kept his eyes on the road. He had no interest in being friends.

RING.

Paul's phone rang inside Mark's pocket. Everyone held their breath while the banjo continued in a ruthless fashion. Then the rest of the band came in right on cue to play in perfect upbeat harmony. It was a beautiful song that would have been enjoyable if not for the situation, or the ringing phone.

"Can I at least see who it is?" Paul asked.

Mark scanned the screen. "Emily."

"Emily?"

"Yes, Emily."

"That's my wife."

"Is she going to be calling the police if she can't get ahold of you?"

"Ex-wife. I haven't talked to her in three years. Honest. I don't know why she would be calling." Paul looked down at the gauge. "We need to stop for gas soon."

Mark leaned over for a look. The needle hovered over empty. He sat back in his seat and grilled Paul with a detective's eye. Then he turned to his family.

"Alright, we're going to stop." Mark smiled at Kelsey. "Everyone should use the bathroom and buy snacks. Candy and chocolate included."

"Bad idea," Paul insisted. "Someone will recognize you."

"Do you really think so?" Mark struggled to

fully grasp the situation he found himself in. "You didn't recognize us."

"I only heard on the radio. Your faces will be all over the TV by now. Someone will recognize you. Definitely. Absolutely. No doubt about it." A sense of satisfaction seemed to leave Paul's lips as he spoke the words.

"My life is ruined!" James yelled.

"What do you suggest then?" Mark asked.

"I suggest you stay in the car. I'll go inside."

Mark laughed. "Stay in the car? You go inside? You heard on the radio that I was a scientist, right? Not a complete moron?"

"I'd say you veer between both."

The pistol was still aimed at Paul as he slowed down and turned into the gas station on the corner. He pulled up alongside a pump and parked. No other cars were around, but Mark's head remained on a swivel, expecting one at any moment.

Paul jumped out of the car and sprinted to the convenience store.

"Shit!" Mark muttered. "He took the keys."

Paul shouted at the cashier inside and pointed to the car. Mark leaped out, and a few more bullets fell from his pocket. He ignored them and opened the back door. "Out. Everyone out." Claire ushered the kids and pierced her husband with a glance. "Quick, quick, quick."

A blue Cadillac pulled into the station. The driver took up two parking spaces and strolled into the store like he owned the place. So much so that he left the engine running unattended.

Mark gazed up to the sky. "Sorry I ever

doubted you." He grabbed Kelsey's arm and headed toward the Cadillac. "Come on! Get in! Now!"

Everyone jumped into the car, but Claire hesitated. "Are you sure about this?"

"We don't have time, Claire." Mark helped her inside and closed the door. He sat in the low-riding driver's seat. Its position seemed more convenient for a nap than for driving. He could barely see over the steering wheel, so he pressed the automatic switch to raise it to a proper level, but it was slow. Painfully slow.

"Hey!" The Cadillac's owner stood in front of the station with an unlit cigarette hanging from his mouth. "Get out of my whip!"

Mark threw the car into drive with the seat half-adjusted and peeled away. The owner cursed and shook his fist behind them as Mark finished adjusting the seat and aligned the mirrors. He modified each mirror to perfection regardless of how long it took. He figured he might need them more than usual.

When he was done, he rested his hand on Claire's. She was shaking, but the warmth of his palm seemed to help. He looked at her. A single tear rolled from her eye and down her cheek. Mark wiped it clean but said nothing.

He still had no real plan, only a word. Canada. But he felt solace in having that, even if that's *all* he had.

10:24 am.

THE ROAD

They drove for nearly an hour without incident. No conversation either.

The radio played on a low volume, and they took country roads to avoid busier ones. The type of roads where you rarely passed other vehicles. No wandering eyes to recognize their worried faces. Or so he hoped.

"Are we going to talk about the gun?" Claire asked.

"I bought it a year ago."

"When were you going to tell me?"

"I never planned to use it."

"When were you going to tell me?"

"I don't know. I'm sorry. It's a good thing I had it, you have to admit."

"Have you shot it?"

"Yes."

"Besides today."

"A couple of times."

"Where?"

"The range."

"Which one?"

A long pause. "Today was the first time."

Claire sighed and looked away. "I just wish I knew. We used to tell each other everything."

She turned up the volume and heard static, so she changed it. An epic guitar solo thrashed the speakers. Then more static. Then an angry rapper shouting about guns. The next turn brought a soulful jazz trumpet solo.

"What's that one channel that plays Christmas music all year long?" she asked.

"Christmas music?" Mark looked at her. "Right now?"

"Let's pretend we're on vacation. We barely even listen to Christmas music on Christmas anymore. And the holidays are not that far away." Claire faced the children. "What do you think?"

"A permanent vacation to Canada in hiding?" James asked sarcastically. "Why not?"

"I don't think anyone wants to listen to Christmas music, Claire," Mark said.

But Claire did not quit. "How about you, Kelsey?"

Kelsey nodded with encouragement, so Claire smiled and continued her search. "How long do you think it will take us on these back roads?"

Mark looked at the clock. 11:17 am. "Before night."

"Then what?"

"I think we should take this one step at a time, sweetie."

"One step at a time?" James butted in. "We're fugitives on the run from the United States government. A middle-class family of four. No, wait, sorry, *upper*-class family of four. I mean, our house is, *was*, not much smaller than my high school. I imagine I don't attend school anymore? No more baseball either."

Kelsey started crying again. Claire scolded James, and he sighed and comforted his sister. Claire searched for the Christmas channel with more vigor.

Bluegrass. Static. Static. Disco. Static. Classical. Static. Blues. Electronic. Static. Static. Alternative. Static.

And then there it was.

"Oh what fun it is to ride in a one-horse open sleigh."

"Are we really going to listen to this right now, Mom?" James asked.

"Jingle bells, jingle bells, jingle all the way."

Mark peered in the rearview mirror and saw Kelsey wiping away her tears and enjoying the song. "I think we can listen to it for a little while, James." His smile found Claire's, and faint glimpses of happiness crept through the cracks.

They drove on and on while Christmas music played and played. Most of the classics. One after another.

"I need to go to the bathroom," Kelsey said.

"Bad?" Mark asked. Kelsey nodded in the rearview. He sighed. "One or two?"

"Both."

Mark drove to the next gas station, but it was ten minutes away and Kelsey was getting antsy. 11:54 am. They pulled into the lot and parked in the farthest spot.

Kelsey wanted to jump out, but James held her

back. "Hold on there, sis."

"It's an emergency!" she replied.

Mark's head shifted around in search of something out of place. Anything.

Claire gazed back to Kelsey and saw pure agony on her young face. She rushed out the door and grabbed her daughter by the wrist. They ran toward the convenience store under Mark's watchful eye. They plowed through the doors.

"Do you need to go?" Mark asked James.

"I'm good," he said. "Lay off the Christmas music for a bit, will you?"

Mark turned it off. Someone walked by the car, and Mark hid his face. James laughed.

"So this is it, huh? This is the rest of our lives?"

"It won't always be like this, James."

"What will it be like, Dad?"

"We will figure it out."

"You keep saying that, but what does that mean? You will figure out what? How to defeat the United States government?"

"James, please."

"Dad, we're screwed... admit it. Screwed!"

Mark stumbled over his words and bit his tongue. He was barely a father to his son in the first place, not since his job took over most of the hours in the day. Their relationship was only on paper, and this was the most time they had spent together in years.

The silence was torturous.

Claire and Kelsey ran out of the store as if being chased by wolves. The cashier followed behind, shouting and yelling.

"Shit," Mark muttered.

Claire and Kelsey hopped into the car and slammed the doors.

"Go! Go!"

Mark peeled out of the station and fired back onto the road. The cashier stepped into the store a defeated man.

"He recognized you?"

"Nope. Bathrooms are for customers only, and I promised we would buy something when we came out."

Mark laughed. "And he was *that* upset?"

"What a stupid rule anyway," Kelsey added.

"What if he did recognize you?" James asked.

"It was just because of the bathroom," Claire replied. "Just the bathroom."

Mark could read the lingering doubts on her face as she turned the music back on.

THE POLICE

"Good tidings we bring to you and your kin."

Claire turned it up three notches. 12:13 pm.

"We wish you a merry Christmas and a happy New Year!"

Mark tapped his fingers on the wheel and smiled. For a brief moment, he nearly forgot why he was driving. Why they were headed to Canada.

WHOOP, WHOOP.

Red and blue sirens flashed in the rearview mirror. A police car was right on their tail. Mark was reminded quickly and turned down the music.

"Shit," Mark whispered.

"Oh my God," Claire said. "Oh my God. Oh my God. Maybe the store clerk did recognize us?"

"It's the car," he said. "It was called in."

"What are we going to do?" Claire asked.

"Are you kidding me?" James wrapped his arms around Kelsey. "Pull over, Dad! This has gotten ridiculous."

"You're right, James." Mark switched his blinker on. "You're right."

Relief washed over Claire's face as he pulled onto the shoulder and stopped. She'd wanted to say it herself but always found excuses to support her husband. She had been doing it for years.

The police officer pulled over behind them, but remained in the cruiser, waiting.

Mark watched him carefully in the mirror.

"He's waiting for backup."

"Backup?" Claire asked.

"He knows who we are," Mark shifted his eyes from the mirror to the open road, from the open road to the mirror.

He remembered his own pistol tucked in his waistband. He remembered the M16s in his face, in all their faces, and what the men said they would do if they spoke to the police. He remembered a lot. All at once.

He could not let that happen.

The cop suddenly exited the car with his gun drawn. He approached the vehicle with extreme caution. He looked young and too anxious to wait for backup to arrive. He wanted to be the hero.

Mark threw the car into drive and slammed on the gas. The car peeled away as the cop raised his weapon but decided against firing at a car with children inside and ran back to his cruiser to pursue them.

"What the hell are you doing?" James yelled.

"Mark…" Claire said. "What *are* you doing?"

"We are going to be alright. Okay? You have to trust me. We are going to be just fine."

He gripped the steering wheel tighter and glanced into his mirror at the chasing vehicle. It gained quickly. It was much faster than the Cadillac, but the stolen car was no slouch.

"Can we get off, please?" James comforted his sister. "We want to live. And not in jail."

"You will not go to jail..." Claire said. "Only your father will."

Mark ignored it all and focused on his driving. He felt like a new man. Like he was capable of anything. He turned up the volume of the music to drown everything out.

"Deck the halls with boughs of holly, FA LA LA LA LA LA LA LA LA! 'Tis the season to be jolly, FA LA LA LA LA LA LA LA LA!"

Claire turned it down. "I don't want to listen to this anymore."

Mark changed it instantly. Static. The next was static too. Then classic rock. A hard-hitting electric guitar riff.

A smile washed over his face. His eyes brightened at the sight of a dirt road up ahead.

Another idea filled his mind. It had not rained in days. The dirt would be dry and dusty.

"What do you guys want for lunch?" Mark asked.

"Are you kidding me?" James said. "My father is a lunatic."

"He is not," Claire defended, but with less conviction than her husband had hoped.

"First place we see, we stop," Mark said. "How about that?"

"How can we stop, dear?" Claire asked.

"With brakes, honey."

"I mean, with the *police*."

"They won't be on our tail long." Mark cut the wheel sharply onto the dirt road, and the cop had to turn around to catch up.

The small head start allowed the Cadillac to kick up a massive cloud of dust behind them before the cop was back on their tail.

The view from the mirror returned the smile on Mark's face. He could no longer see the cruiser, which meant the cruiser could no longer see him.

He cut the wheel again, but with no turning road in sight. His family screamed as the Cadillac flew into tall grass before striking a tree.

The impact deployed the airbags.

"What the hell, Mark?" Claire yelled. "Are you crazy?" He looked at her with a finger over his lips, asking for quiet as the airbags deflated.

Sirens darted through the giant cloud of dust and straight past them.

Mark put the car in reverse. It still worked, despite the sizable dent in the front end. He backed up onto the road as the dust began to settle. He shifted into drive and traveled back the way they came.

"Now we can get lunch," Mark said.

Kelsey vomited all over the backseat.

"Ahh! Nasty!" James said.

"I have a headache." Kelsey wiped her mouth and chin of dribble.

"Me too," James added.

"I think we all do," Mark admitted. "But we need to keep going. The officer will be turning around soon, and backup will not be far. We need a new car, and fast."

"Honey…" Claire looked at him as if she didn't even recognize him. "You're scaring me."

"And I think a little food in our bellies would do us all wonders."

THE SWAP

12:22 pm. Mark kept his eyes glued on the rearview mirror. He took a right at the first intersection he saw. Then a left, then another right. 12:25 pm. No sign of the police.

A single brown sign with white lettering and the symbol a hiker caught Mark's eye.

WHITE CREEK NEXT RIGHT.

"Where are we going now?" Claire asked.

"Getting a new car."

"Just like *that*?"

"Sort of."

The long dirt road led to a small parking area for the trailhead. Four parked vehicles occupied the lot. 12:27 pm.

The family exited the car and were thankful for it. Mark sized up the four other vehicles. The third one he tried was unlocked. It was an old, beat-up van with little inside except a second row of seats, a tapestry-filled interior, and a strong marijuana smell.

He searched the center console but found nothing. He checked the driver's-side visor mirror and out fell the keys. He showed them off like a lost treasure.

"Got to love hippies," he said. "So trusting. What are you waiting for?"

Rustling brush caused Mark and the rest of the family to freeze. It was only a whitetail deer and not the owner of the van they were stealing. The animal looked over and scurried away as if it sensed danger.

"Come on!" Mark said.

They sprang into the van and drove back onto the road. Mark remained at the speed limit to arouse zero suspicion. 12:34 pm.

"I don't know about you guys, but I really need to eat," he insisted. "I'm starving."

A police helicopter flew overhead but kept going.

Sighs of relief.

THE DINER

The wheels of the van stopped. 1:27pm. Mark looked to Claire and the children, but they all faced the other side of the dirt parking lot, where a diner sat.

THEO'S DINER.

The restaurant appeared like a tiny island in a vast sea of dirt and rock. The parking lot had the capacity to accommodate hundreds, but the diner sat no more than thirty. Claire turned to Mark with troubled eyes. Her lips quivered, and she uttered her next words softly.

"This is not a good idea, Mark. They will recognize us."

"This is the first place we've seen in a long time," he reminded her. "There's not much on these roads, and I cannot drive another mile without something in my stomach."

"Then I'll drive," James said. "Straight to the police station."

"No, I will," Claire insisted.

"Neither of you are driving. And we are *not* going to the police." Mark jerked his head toward the diner. "There are two trucks and one car outside.

They probably don't even have a TV in there. Plus, you said the convenience store clerk didn't recognize you, right?"

"I don't know, Mark." Claire's voice cracked. "Customers have TVs at home. What happens when they come in? We were on the radio too. They have given detailed descriptions of us. Of our family. They probably know everything about us. Oh my God, Mark, what are we going to do? How are we going to live?"

"Look." Mark held her hand. "I will walk in first and feel it out. Only if everything is fine, nothing fishy at all, perfectly average, will I come back to the van for the three of you. Okay? Does that sound good?"

"Couldn't you just get the food to go?"

"We should sit down for a meal as a family," Mark said.

"It might be the last time." She began to cry.

Mark rubbed her hand as if it shivered with cold, but it was warm, clammy. He gazed at the diner and then back to his wife. "It will *not* be the last time. But rather, one of the more memorable ones. That's all. Memorable. We'll be joking about this one for years."

Claire shot him a glance, her patience wearing thin.

"We've all had a *very* long day. That's why we should *all* sit down and eat a meal together… like a family."

"We barely ate as a family before," James chimed in. "Not since that stupid job."

"I'll go in first and talk to the waitress," Mark

continued. "If she recognizes me, I'll be able to tell."

"How?" James said.

"Based on my read." Mark found it harder and harder to ignore his son's constant negativity. "I'll either come out in a calm stroll or a mad sprint." Mark smiled, but no one else did. He leaned over and wiped away Claire's tears and kissed her on the forehead.

"I don't know, Mark," she said.

"We eat this meal and then head straight to the Canadian border." Mark wiped another tear from her cheek. "Okay?"

Claire nodded.

Mark turned to the children. "Okay?"

Kelsey nodded, but not James.

"We will be fine. You have to trust me." Mark stepped into the crisp air. It filled his nostrils and soothed him. He found his wife's eyes once more. He had never seen her so scared. The children too. The same went for him.

He tried strolling calmly across the massive dirt lot, but his heart pounded in his chest.

He wished he could offer a better explanation for the meal, but he thought it best he didn't. The police chase gave him perspective. His time with them was limited. He would not be able to control his fate, but what he could control was his place in the family. Husband and father. The provider. And he wanted to have a family meal.

He needed it.

DING.

He entered the diner and set off the bell. It

smelled like every diner did: coffee and grilled food.

Two men sat at the counter on opposite ends, but the five booths were all empty. A single waitress poured one of the men coffee and looked up.

"Hello, sir!" she greeted.

"Hello," Mark responded.

"Just you?"

"No, my family's in the car."

One of the men at the counter found Mark's eyes. It was brief but intense. The stranger turned back around and sipped his coffee.

"Are they not hungry?" she asked.

"No, they are."

"Well, then, what are they doing in the car?" She giggled.

"Uhh…" Mark stuttered. "My daughter wanted to know if you had ice cream."

"Ice cream?" The waitress smiled. "Well, of course we have ice cream."

"Great," Mark replied. "I'll let her know."

He walked back out but paused in the doorway and gazed all around the diner. No television in sight. No radio either. But music played softly in the background. Where did it come from?

"Something else, sir?" the waitress asked.

"What's playing the music?"

The waitress smiled and presented an old record player spinning a vinyl behind the counter. "My father's old record player," she said. "Much better than the radio."

Mark nodded and left. His smile grew as he

walked back to the van. They might be able to pull this off.

He returned to his family with the information needed to convince them out of the van, and it only took five minutes.

"Try not to look so weird," Mark told them. "We're just a family passing through on a road trip. An ordinary family, which you guys are not acting like."

"This is bullshit, Dad," James said.

"Watch your mouth in front of your sister," Mark replied.

"Are you kidding me? You can be involved in high-speed police chases but I can't swear? Jesus Christ, you've lost it, Dad."

Mark stopped and grabbed James firmly by the arm. He yanked him back toward the van, to his son's displeasure.

"What the hell?" James struggled. "What gives? What did I do?"

"We'll be just a minute," Mark assured the waiting Claire and Kelsey.

"What the hell's your problem, Dad?" James rubbed his sore arm.

"What's my problem?" Mark took a deep breath. "You. You're my problem."

"What?"

"I said, 'You're my problem.' Right now, *you* are my problem. Everyone is *thinking* the things you are saying, but it helps nothing. I'm trying to keep this family together… against all odds. And *you* are not helping. Not at all. Quite the opposite, in fact. It's like you're trying to break up the family."

"I am not trying to break up the family," James said. "Don't be so dramatic."

"But son, this is dramatic. You should know that better than your sister. Maybe even better than your mother. Our situation is very serious. You heard the radio earlier. My coworker and his family were killed, but we weren't. Is it because they went to the police and we didn't? I think so. That's why we can't go to the police, son. You need to understand that."

"Then what do we do?"

"I really don't know. That's why I want to go to Canada. To buy us some time so that I, *we*, can think about what to do next. But in the meantime, I need to keep this family together. *We* need to keep this family together, and it starts with this meal, at this diner, at this time."

James wanted to speak but hesitated.

"Being a father is the only thing I can control right now, son," Mark said. "I lost control of it over the last few years. No... I always had control, but I ignored it. I want to do better while I still have a chance. We used to be so close."

Water swelled in Mark's eyes and his son's too.

"Help me be a father again."

James hugged him with strong arms. Mark could see Claire watching from a distance and she smiled. The moment was sweet.

The family regrouped and entered the diner.

DING.

The waitress's head flicked up again. Both men at the counter turned.

"There they are!" the waitress said. "Welcome!"

"Thank you," Mark replied.

"Hi," James added with an awkward wave. He shared a glance with his father. At least he was trying.

"Well, hello there, young man. Would you folks like to sit at one of the booths?"

"That would be great." Mark shuffled his family into the corner one and sat near the window with the best view of the road.

"I'll have menus and silverware with you right away." The waitress topped off the coffee for the other man.

After Mark was happy with his angle of the street, he moved his attention to the two men at the counter.

One wore faded leather. The other a long brown coat. They sipped their coffee and minded their own business. Or so it seemed.

"This is nice, huh?" James looked over to his sister. Sadness still consumed her. He put his arm around her shoulder and pulled her in close. "I bet they even have French toast here. All diners do."

A smile slipped onto her face.

"French toast?" Mark said. "That sounds pretty good actually. Breakfast for lunch. What do we say?"

"Yes!" Kelsey responded.

"Absolutely," James said.

"Let's do it." Claire finally smiled.

The waitress came with menus and silverware as promised. "How are y'all doing this afternoon?"

she asked. "My name is Charlene, and I'll be serving you this afternoon. What can I start y'all off with?" She laid out each item on the table with what looked like too many years of practice.

"We were thinking breakfast," Mark said.

"Excellent choice, sir. Breakfast is our specialty. That menu is on the back."

Everyone flipped the menu in harmony.

"Drinks or water to start?" Charlene asked.

"Definitely water. And coffee. Lots of coffee." Mark looked to the others.

"Coffee for me as well," Claire said.

"And you two sweethearts?"

"Just water, please," James said.

"Chocolate milkshake," Kelsey said. James nudged her. "Please."

"A milkshake *and* ice cream?" Charlene said with a friendly smile, but Kelsey had no idea what she was talking about, so the waitress quickly moved on. "Well, I'll get those drinks right away and be back for your breakfast orders."

Claire thanked the waitress as she left. "This *is* nice, Mark. Thank you for convincing us to come in."

He smiled. "You're welcome."

The family looked over the menus and discussed what they wanted. French toast was unanimous, and soon Charlene returned with a full tray balanced over her shoulder. Four glasses of water, two empty mugs, and one tall chocolate milkshake. Each one was accompanied by a *hun*, *sug*, or *sweetheart*.

The coffee pot was last, and Charlene poured

while tucking the tray underneath her armpit. "Do y'all know what you're having?"

"Yes," Mark replied. "We are all having Theo's Frenchie. Two with bacon, two with sausage."

"Great choices." Charlene wrote nothing down. "Anything else?"

"That will be it, thank you," Mark said.

Charlene looked up at the window and hesitated. "Would you look at that…" Mark jerked his neck to the window. "It's snowing!" she finished. "First one of the year. Well, *this* part of the year, at least. Isn't snow lovely? I love it. Love the way it looks."

Scattered white flakes danced gently onto the dirt lot. Charlene left with their orders, but Mark's eyes remained glued on the window.

And not because of the snow.

A pickup truck raced down the road toward the diner and skidded in a hurry. The driver jumped out and rushed inside.

DING.

"Hey, Bill," Charlene greeted. "What's the big hurry?"

"You haven't heard?" Bill replied. "Put on the damn radio!"

Charlene stopped the record player and pulled an old radio from behind the counter and blew off the dust. She turned it on. Static. She played with the dial and antennas until she found something. A reporter.

"The destruction is incredible. We have never seen anything like it. The death toll is estimated to be about twenty thousand, but those numbers are only speculation. And optimistic speculation. It will be days before we fully realize the final death toll and damage. Just unbelievable. One thing is clear, ladies and gentlemen. This is the single deadliest attack on American soil. Ever. Bigger than Pearl Harbor. Bigger than 9/11. And again in New York City."

The family stared at Mark, but he avoided their glares. He kept his eyes on Bill.

The reporter on the radio continued.

"It is believed the missing chemicals reported earlier this morning, Sulfuric Nine and Hydrochloric Five, have a connection with the attack. Experts believe those two chemicals could have been used in this type of bomb."

Bill found Mark's gaze. His mouth nearly dropped to the floor as he pointed toward the family, gasping for words.

Charlene was too focused on the radio and her own crying to notice. Claire and Kelsey began crying too. James looked to his father for direction as his eyes watered and he gulped.

"Mark Frasier is the prime suspect," the reporter went on, "and is still at large, presumably traveling with his family."

The two men at the counter turned.

"Dad?" James asked.

Charlene finally noticed Bill and looked over to their table. All eyes were on the family as the reporter listed details that matched in every way.

"Dad, we should go," James said.

Mark shook the reporter's voice from his head and rushed his family out of the booth.

"Hey!" Bill shouted. "You're Mark Frasier! You did this! You killed those people, you son of a bitch!"

Mark pushed Bill out of the way and knocked him over. He ushered his family out of the diner and slammed the door shut. He slid the outdoor bench underneath the door handle just in time for it to push and shake with force.

The Frasiers sprinted across the expansive parking lot and hopped into the van. The bench gave way, and the door swung open.

Mark sped back onto the road while Bill ran to his truck and gave chase.

The snowfall continued. 1:53 pm.

THE VIGILANTE

Mark kept a close eye on the rearview mirror. Bill tailed them for several minutes but never raised a cell phone to his ear and did not seem like the type with a Bluetooth. For now, it was only them.

The snow worsened. 2:01 pm.

"What now?" Claire finally asked.

"We are going to isolate him so he cannot get help." Mark turned onto another road.

"Dad?" James asked as he comforted Kelsey.

"What exactly do you plan to do, Mark?" Claire asked worriedly.

"I am not going to kill the guy!" he shouted. "Jeez, come on. I'm just going to talk to him. I think he will understand that we are a good American family, but we need to isolate ourselves from the main road and nearby roads because the waitress more than likely called the police and told them which direction we were headed."

Claire buried her face in her hands.

"They will not only sweep the main road but the connecting ones too," he said. "And we can expect more helicopters. We need to go a little farther. *And* we'll need to take another route to the border. They'll know we are headed to Canada."

Mark drove the van down four more roads before feeling comfortable enough to stop. Bill was close behind the entire way, and when Mark pulled over, he followed. Claire grabbed her husband by the wrist before he could leave the van.

"Are you sure you know what you're doing?" she asked.

"Yes, I am sure."

"Okay. Be safe." She turned to the children. "And you two... Be on your best behavior. Be polite and smile."

"What do you mean?" James asked.

"They're not coming with me, Claire," Mark said.

"They will help you win him over," she said.

"Just let me speak with him," he insisted.

"You are taking them with you," she said. "James, take your sister and go with your father."

"No, James. Stay in the van."

"Dammit, Mark! You need to convince this man that you are not responsible for the greatest attack on American soil even though everyone on the television and radio says you are. You need all the help you can get. Two cute American kids will surely help, and it will surely help me from not having a freakin' panic attack."

She caught her breath while James and Kelsey silently stepped out of the van and joined their father.

They walked over to the truck, where Bill waited with a shotgun rested on the open window frame of the driver's-side door.

"Slower!" he yelled. They obeyed.

"My name is Mark Frasier."

"I know!" Bill shouted. "I'm taking you in!"

"I wanted to tell you my side of the story and why we're here."

"Not interested! Get your hands up!"

Mark raised his hands in the air. The children too. "Please, sir," Mark pleaded, "I beg of you. Listen to our story."

"Shut up! I said *not interested!*"

"Do you have a family, sir?" James asked, but the question was ignored.

"Shut it!"

"Please, mister," Kelsey added. "Please."

Bill hesitated. His eyes moved to the children and landed on young Kelsey. The gun shook in his hands.

"Well?" Bill asked.

"Well…" Mark peered at James and Kelsey on either side of him but kept his hands in the air. "It's because of these two. And my wife who is sitting in the van. The three of them."

"Think I won't shoot you in front of your family?"

"Yes." Mark replied.

"I will."

"I was hoping you were the kind of guy that would only use the gun to command the situation and not for shooting."

"You thought wrong."

"I don't think I did."

"So, your wife and two kids?" Bill asked.

"My wife and two kids were held hostage by a

group of armed men. I don't know their names or who they were but they targeted my family because of my job. I work for Valine Corp. Or worked. They design and produce new chemicals for manufacturing, but lately most of the work was for the government. We began developing chemical mutations."

"Yeah, yeah, tell me what I don't know, scum."

"These men shoved semi-automatic rifles into the faces of my family and told me if I didn't go into the Valine facility early this morning and deliver as many barrels of Sulfuric Nine as I could by 8 am then my family would be raped and killed. Worse, actually, but I'll leave it at that. So, I drove to work this morning and did as they demanded."

"You killed twenty thousand people."

"I did what I had to do to save my family. I didn't know they would make a bomb."

"Angry men with rifles stealing dangerous chemicals don't sound like the kind of men who would make a bomb?"

"I—I…" Mark stuttered.

"How will you live with yourself?" Bill spat on the ground.

"The bomb could have been anything." James defended his father. "Plus, there's no evidence that Sulfuric Nine was used in the attack, right? Experts *believe* the connection, but the connection is only coincidence. You said you delivered the barrels at 8 am?"

Mark nodded.

"And when was the attack?" James asked. "1:30 the latest?"

"1:07," Bill corrected.

"1:07. Even earlier," James said. "That's a quick turnaround from barreled chemicals leaving a lab in Pennsylvania to a bomb detonating all the way in New York City."

The silence overwhelmed the scene, and Bill loosened his grip on the shotgun as snow collected on the long barrel.

"What do you think they will use the Sulfuric Nine for?" Bill asked.

"I don't know," Mark replied.

"Nothing good, I presume? What if it is the same group? This was just the small bomb."

"I hope you're wrong."

"I hope so too." He lowered the shotgun and moved his finger away from the trigger. "Why don't you go to the police?"

"We're afraid." Mark looked again to his children. "They told us that if we do, they will find us. Look what happened to the other guy."

"Henry something." Bill pondered. "You reckon he went to the cops?"

"I think so."

"So, you ran."

"Yes."

"I *do* have a family." Bill looked down at the snowy ground. "Four sons, two daughters, twelve grandchildren. I reckon I might do the same as you. But that don't make it right. Not in God's eyes. He'll be the final judge and see the debts are paid."

"Did you call the police?" Mark asked.

"No cellphone." Bill placed the shotgun in his truck. "Those things are a bunch of racket, if you ask me. Make it right with God, and do the right thing."

"What is the right thing?" Mark asked.

"You'll know. But I won't have anything to do with it." He climbed inside his truck and drove away with an expression of regret.

Mark nodded and walked his children back to the van and settled them with their relieved mother.

What was the *right* thing? Mark merged onto the snowy road and drove. 2:23 pm.

THE ACCIDENT

More than an inch of snow had accumulated on the sides of the road, and the storm seemed only in its infancy.

Still no sign of police. 2:43 pm.

"Do you think they've reported the van stolen yet?" Claire asked.

"Depends how long their hike was." Mark smiled but wiped it clean when he saw his wife's expression. He opened the center console. "Did you see a phone anywhere? Check the glove compartment. Maybe it's in there."

Claire searched and found exactly that. A cell phone. She showed it to her husband and his smile returned.

"Well, they won't call the police immediately at least," Mark said.

"This isn't funny, Mark."

"Throw it out the window."

"What?"

"Throw it out the window," he repeated. "Come on. It'll feel good, and they won't be able to track us."

Claire manually rolled the window down, and

snow blew in. She took the phone and threw it as far as she could. It did feel good.

"What if the waitress offered descriptions of the vehicle? The plates?"

"We parked far from the diner. No way she saw the plates. I think we will be fine." Mark turned the windshield wiper dial one more click as the storm raged on. "I cannot explain why, I just feel that way. And we'll need gas soon. *And* I'm still starving. We'll need to find a way to get food. I want my breakfast. We should still have our breakfast."

Red lights appeared around the bend. The snowy conditions did not offer much visibility, but it looked like a long line of cars.

It was traffic at a dead stop.

Mark pulled up behind the last car. "Must be an accident." He gazed around as snow collected on the trees and branches, on the grasses and plants. "Christmas music would be more appropriate now."

Claire chuckled, and Mark fished for the radio channel.

Static. Static. News.

"At least twenty thousand are confirmed dead," the reporter said. "Many more deaths are expected to be confirmed in the coming days."

Mark changed the channel.

"I am reporting live near Ground Zero of what's already being described as the worst attack in the history of the United States."

Switch. Static. Switch.

"I am here with Jeff Henderson, who was four blocks from the explosions when they happened, and he's here to tell his story. It's incredible, so brace yourself."

Mark turned off the radio. "No music, I guess."

A police cruiser rushed past alongside the traffic with flashing lights. Mark flinched, but the vehicle was gone as soon as it arrived.

"Hopefully they get it cleared up soon." Claire opened the glove compartment. "But here, I saw this when I was looking for the phone." She placed the unmarked disc into the player. Track one played.

"Hello, friend," a calm voice with an accent said. "My name is Jim San Jen Son, and I want to welcome you to my little patch of this patch of existence. A patch of meditation, yoga and fasting. A peaceful patch."

Mark turned to Claire and burst into laughter. She and the children joined. For a moment, they seemed to be having fun. Mark turned it up.

"I could tell you about my certifications, years of experience and my personal retreat with the Dalai Lama. I could go on about my Everest expedition without oxygen or spending two years in an Antarctic camp while fasting, but this disc is not about me. It's about you. Every single one of *you*."

The family laughed harder the longer it played.

"But it's also about me. And how I can help you achieve those dreams you dreamed. Even the dreams that were undreamable. The undreamable dreams that you dreamed to dream can be achieved today. Or maybe tomorrow. But first, keep listening."

Suddenly, Mark stopped laughing. Religion,

spirituality, yoga, meditation, herbal remedies, all of it used to be hogwash to him. He was a firm believer in hard science, and that was it. But not anymore. After today, he found himself questioning everything he ever knew.

"And no, this is not a dream," the voice continued. "This is as real as it gets. But even if it was a dream, we could make it real. Together. By listening."

Mark listened intently.

"Clear your mind, my friend. Clear it of all the clutter that keeps it spinning day after day after day. Clear it of everything that stops you from enjoying your life. Clear it of everything. Your troubles, your problems, your stress. Everything. Clear it and keep it clear."

HONK, HONK.

"Mark?" Claire said. "Cars are moving."

He pressed the gas and caught back up, then followed the line of slow-moving traffic alongside the accident. Three police vehicles, two fire engines and one ambulance created a spectacle for the passing drivers. But only a single car was involved in the crash.

It appeared to have struck an old oak tree at the end of its swerving. The hood and front of the vehicle were blackened by a fire that had since been extinguished. One wheel had flown off, and the front axle was ripped apart. Engine pieces were scattered everywhere under the falling snow.

Traffic passed with caution and curiosity.

"Do you think they survived?" Kelsey asked.

"I don't think so, sweetie," Mark replied

honestly. "The ambulance is still here."

A police officer waved traffic on.

"Get down." Mark zipped up his jacket all the way to the top and pushed his mouth and cheeks into the collar. He felt and looked ridiculous, like a turtle hiding in his shell. The kids ducked down into the leg space of the back seats while Claire froze in the passenger seat.

The cop watched each car pass, but Mark looked straight at the road ahead. He stared at the windshield as if his life depended on it. He thought it did.

They passed the officer and all the commotion without a fuss. Traffic picked back up, and they were off again. 2:58 pm.

"Now exhale deeply and keep that mind clear," Jim San Jen Son suggested. "Relieve all the stress, my friend. Relieve all the tension and move on with your life. Move on to a good life. Your new life."

THE STATION

The gas station came after twenty-five minutes and nineteen miles. The snow became sporadic and unpredictable. The intensity fluctuated and the wind too. They had passed a large sign a few miles back.

CANADA 100 MILES.

Mark pulled up alongside a pump behind a minivan. He quickly zipped his jacket up to his nose and looked around to see if anyone was paying attention to the old van.

They weren't.

"I'll go in with cash and fill up first." Mark opened his wallet and counted. "In case we need to leave in a hurry, gas is priority. When I go in for a second time for my change, I will pick up food, because I am about fifteen minutes away from eating the nuts and bolts off this damn van."

Kelsey giggled, and it broke the tension. Claire smiled softly.

"Everyone else will stay in the van," he said. "Don't look out the windows. Don't make eye contact with anyone."

"Does anyone need the bathroom again?" Claire asked.

"I think it would be better to stay in the van," Mark said.

"So, the most recognizable face goes in? You look ridiculous like that."

"I'm not going in like this." Mark stepped out and opened the trunk doors of the van. "There must be something else to help."

Tent, sleeping bags, blankets and a duffel bag. He searched the bag and pulled one item out. A red scarf with white lettering across it.

YOU'LL NEVER WALK ALONE.

He had no idea what it meant, but it gave him the creeps. Like he was being watched. He wrapped it around his neck and face and positioned it with great care.

"I'm visiting from Florida." He smiled underneath the fabric. "Not used to the cold."

The woman filling up the minivan seemed to watch, so Mark waited until she went back to her task before shifting his handgun to the back of his waistband.

"I will be right back." He closed the trunk and walked to the small convenience store one step at a time.

The diner did not work out, but he still needed this. He still needed to give his family this. He still needed to be a father again.

RING.

The bell above the door was painfully loud. He approached the counter, as cool as ever.

"Cold out there, is it?" The cashier smirked.

"Yes," Mark's muffled voice replied. "I'm visiting from Florida." He walked up to the counter.

"Nice scarf," the man said.

"Thank you." Mark paused and, for a second, forgot the pump number. Pump 1? No, that was the woman with the minivan. Pump 2. It was pump 2.

"Pump 2. Forty on pump 2."

The cashier pressed a couple of buttons on the register, and it popped open. He placed the two twenties into the drawer and slammed it shut. The impact startled Mark.

"Forty on pump 2, man. Anything else?"

"Uhh…" Mark's voice cracked. "No, not right now. Thank you." He turned and walked as fast as he could back to the van. The minivan had gone, but another car pulled up alongside the third pump.

Mark went to load the nozzle into the tank but realized he was parked on the wrong side. He closed his eyes in frustration and drifted back to Jim San Jen Son.

Relieve all the stress, my friend. Relieve all the tension and move on with your life. Move on to a good life. Your new life.

He breathed deeply and placed the nozzle back into its slot. He stepped into the van and turned the engine on.

"What's going on?" Claire asked.

"I need to turn around," Mark responded.

"Turn around?"

"Yes."

Claire suddenly realized why, and it brought a smile to her face. "The tank is on the other side, isn't it?"

"Yes."

Claire laughed, and the children joined in. Even

Mark laughed as he repositioned the van to fill it properly. It cost $31.48 and took seven full minutes. Country stations always pumped slow.

The car at the third pump left in a hurry as Mark screwed the gas cap back on. Adjusting the scarf one more time, he signaled two thumbs up to his family and headed back to the store.

The bell atop the door seemed even louder.

"Change?" the cashier asked.

"Food." Marked turned to the two small aisles of bagged snacks and candy. He walked into one of the aisles and browsed. Potato chips, spicy potato chips, curvy potato chips, pretzels, pretzel sticks, pretzel shapes, pretzel chips. But then he remembered something else. Something even more enticing. Breakfast.

He walked around into the next aisle and his eyes lit up. Sugary pastries and packaged snacks. Cinnamon rolls, apple strudels, apple fritters, apple scones, blueberry scones, low-calorie scones, muffins, mini donuts, regular donuts, maple syrup. His smile stretched from ear to ear. Breakfast.

RING.

Mark stopped. His heart thumped. Two hooded men strolled into the store. One black hoodie, one blue. They went to the counter and flicked their heads toward the cigarettes.

Mark scrutinized their every movement. They paid for their packs and left. He watched as they climbed back into their car while the driver attended the pump.

Mark forced his eyes back to the snacks. Breakfast looked so good. He grabbed one of everything. Even the jug of Vermont maple syrup.

He balanced it all in a makeshift pouch he shaped from his jacket and shuffled toward the cashier. He dumped the lot onto the counter, and pastries flew everywhere. They crashed into the lighters, the gum, the licorice and the matches. One even fell to the floor.

"Anything else?" The cashier sighed.

Mark adjusted his scarf and pretended to look around the store one last time before he offered a shake of the head. "No. I think that's it."

The cashier rang up all the items and seemed upset at having to do so. "Would you like a bag?"

RING.

The door swung open. The blue hoodie walked back in. Mark felt his body heating up as if he was wearing five sweaters. All of a sudden, his breath felt like fire underneath the scarf. Like he had eaten the hottest pepper on the planet with no water in sight. The temperature in the convenience store must have reached a thousand degrees.

The man stepped behind him and waited in line.

"That will be $44.59," the cashier said. "Would you like a bag? For a second time."

"Yes." Mark strained to keep from turning around. The presence of the other customer made him uneasy. Mark reached into his wallet and fished for the appropriate sum of cash. "Change on pump 2 as well."

The cashier sighed again. Another task. He jammed the pastries into a thin plastic bag and somehow managed to fit them all. He then punched several more keys on the register. "Your gas was $31.48. Out of forty is $8.52. Out of $44.59 is $36.07. You owe $36.07."

Mark handed him two more twenties. The cashier pressed one button especially hard on the register, and the drawer popped open, to his distaste.

"Hurry up, will ya?" the blue hoodie insisted.

Mark tried to remain calm. He reached out his hand for the change and shoved it into his pocket. Two of the coins dropped. One bounced off the counter and the other flew onto the floor. Both rolled far, but who cared.

Mark rushed toward the door with the bag of pastries. He did everything he could. Everything. But his glance still found the man's. The moment was so intense Mark thought he would faint.

"It's not *that* cold, man." The stranger laughed.

"I'm from Florida." Mark dashed out the door with sweat dripping down his forehead and rushed across the gas station.

HONK.

A truck stopped in front of him. The driver threw his arms up in annoyance as Mark waved his apologies and scurried the rest of the way to the van. He hopped inside and shut the door, out of breath.

"What did you get?" Claire asked.

Mark smiled. "Breakfast."

THE FEAST

They were back on the road. The ripping of packages and wrappers filled the old van. The sweet smell of sugar and frosting tantalized their noses. Mark drove with one hand on the wheel, one hand shoving a glazed donut into his mouth.

"Should we say grace?" Kelsey asked.

Everyone hesitated, and Mark lifted his teeth from the donut. Stomachs growled.

"That's an amazing idea, sweetie," her mother encouraged, but Mark stumbled and could not remember the words. He was the opposite of religious, but Claire insisted on raising the children Catholic. They still rarely said grace before a meal, especially in the last few years. They rarely even ate as a family anymore.

The words came to him.

"Bless us, O Lord, and these, Thy gifts, which we are about to receive from Thy bounty. Through Christ, our Lord. Amen."

"Amen," the rest replied.

The attack on the food commenced. Claire broke off a piece of blueberry scone as if holding on to her manners, but she devoured it quickly and

126

moved on to the next piece. The kids chomped down on cinnamon rolls in chaotic harmony.

Everyone chewed their breakfasts in silence. Crumbs, flakes and icing found their way from lips to fingers to floor. Smiles could be seen through the opening and closing jaws.

Mark had pulled it off.

"This is what we've been missing all day," he said with his mouth full. "This right here. Breakfast. You cannot start the day without breakfast. But we did. That's why the day has been so poor. It's because we hadn't had our breakfast. *Now* we are ready for the day. *Now* we are ready for its challenges. And... only... 3:49 pm. Plenty of day and plenty of challenges left for us to tackle with full stomachs, as a family."

For a moment, the family forgot about the twenty thousand dead.

"What a great idea, Daddy." Kelsey tried wiping the icing from her mouth but only made things worse. James laughed but reached over to help. Claire ate the last piece of scone and smiled. Her satisfaction was the most warming to Mark. Her smile was always the most warming to him, and he had missed its frequency over the years.

A spot of sunlight pierced the clouds and shined down onto the road. Snow swirling in the wind sparkled in the penetrating light.

"Look," Mark said.

Everyone stopped chewing.

"It's beautiful," Claire said.

Mark turned off his headlights and allowed the natural light to take over. The clouds remained open to create the most picturesque moment for the family.

It felt special. It felt special to all of them. Like the changing of their fortunes.

But the clouds closed back up and the storm went on.

"Can you pass the mini donuts?" Kelsey licked her fingers clean of icing while her mother dug into the plastic bag of goodies and passed the mini chocolate-covered donuts. Kelsey needed no invitation to dive in.

"If only we had something to wash it all down with," Mark said. "Like…"

"Chocolate milk!" Kelsey answered.

"Yes! Chocolate milk. More chocolate." Mark chuckled. "But I was thinking Bloody Marys." He glanced at his wife with a smirk.

"A bloody what?" Kelsey asked.

"An adult beverage, hun," Mark said.

"I could use one too," James added shyly.

"James…" Claire said.

"You know what, James," Mark said, "you're seventeen and, after a day like today, you could have a Bloody Mary on my watch." Claire nearly agreed but dared not admit it. "Any scones left?"

"Yes." Claire handed him a raspberry one.

"You said there was an apple fritter, right?" James asked.

"Yes, yes." Claire pulled out a single-packaged apple fritter and tossed it to him. "Any more orders?"

"Remember that night in Disney World all those years ago?" James asked. "When Kelsey ordered two hundred dollars in room service!"

"Blew our food budget in one night," Mark said.

"But how delicious was it?" Kelsey asked.

"Quite delicious, sweetie," Claire said. "What was it? Five big bowls of chicken nuggets and eight sundaes?"

"Two sundaes each," she replied.

Everyone laughed.

"This breakfast comes pretty close to that night," James said.

"I would say," Claire said.

"Even better," Mark said. "And cheaper." Laughter filled the van while the words of Jim San Jen Son repeated again and again in Mark's head.

The calm voice spoke over the one constantly reminding him of the situation. For now.

Relieve all the stress, my friend. Relieve all the tension and move on with your life. Move on to a good life. Your new life.

THE GAME

"I have an idea!" Kelsey proclaimed when everyone had finished eating.

"What's that, honey?" Claire asked.

"Let's play a game."

Smiles filled the van, and it brightened Mark's heart. Everyone was onboard.

"What kind of game, Kels?" James asked.

"Umm... I spy!" She gazed out the window and searched.

"We haven't played that in years." Claire looked at Mark with joy. "Remember the road trips we used to take?"

"Yeah, and remember the last one?" he replied. "How it ended..."

"I spy... a... moose!" Kelsey said.

"What?" Mark looked around like an excited child. "Really? Where?" He looked and he looked but there was nothing. His wife held in a mouthful of laughter.

"Very funny," Mark said.

Kelsey giggled. "Sorry, Daddy."

"Good one, sis." James gave her a high five.

"No more fake spies." Mark settled back in his

seat. "Especially of someone's favorite animal. Only real spies. And that's not how you play the game."

"It was Kelsey's idea," Claire said. "She decides how we play the game."

Kelsey studied the window again. "I spy... an old barn!" Everyone's head rotated in search of the supposed barn.

"Found it!" Claire pointed. And there it was. An old barn in total disrepair tucked away in some pines. They passed it in a flash.

"Your turn, Mom!" Kelsey said.

"Umm..." Claire started. "I... spy... a... pine tree!" The van filled with more laughter.

"Found it!" James proclaimed. He pointed at the grove of pine trees surrounding the road in every direction. "Right there!"

"Nope," Claire replied. "That's not the one."

"Is it that one?" Kelsey pointed.

"Warmer."

"How about that one?" Mark asked.

"Colder."

"It's got to be that one!" James said.

"Yes!" Claire conceded.

"I spy... an apple!" James offered. Mark and Kelsey looked out the window but Claire did not. She gazed around the van.

"Warmer," James said.

"Who?" Mark asked.

"Mom."

"In the van?" Mark sighed. "I have a disadvantage as the driver, you know. How am I supposed to look around the van while I drive?"

"Quit being a baby," Claire replied and held up the torn wrapper of the apple fritter. A picture of a sliced apple was on the logo for all to see.

"Mom got it."

"Let's pick something in front of us, yeah?" Mark asked.

"In front of us?" Claire repeated.

"Please."

"How about…"

Three helicopters roared overhead, and everyone looked out the window. They were headed in the same direction as the van. They were military aircraft.

"How about three helicopters," she finished.

"Well, that's an easy one," Mark admitted as the family stared at the aircraft traveling far into the northern distance. But then they heard the sound of more.

Six more military helicopters followed not far behind the others. Mark's mind scurried back to the terrorists. The cops. The bombs.

"Is that normal?" Kelsey asked.

THE STRETCH

The Frasiers drove on. No more games were played, and time passed slowly.

The helicopters had everyone's heads scrambling, especially Mark's. He found it more and more difficult to remain the cool father he was trying to embody.

The snow steadied to a soft sprinkle as they passed another sign that brightened in the headlights.

CANADA 20 MILES.

"Not too far now." Mark stated the obvious. He said it to get his mind away from the helicopters. It was hard to think about anything else. How much time did he have left with his family? Road congestion picked up and cars seemed to be in a hurry.

Relieve all the stress, my friend. Relieve all the tension and move on with your life. Move on to a good life. Your new life.

"Can we turn some music back on?" James asked. "*Not* Christmas music, please."

"Sure, son." Mark turned on the radio and worked the dial. Static. Static. Static. News. Static.

Back to the news. He could not help it. He was a scientist, after all, and curiosity came with the territory.

"We are seeing widespread panic among citizens after another explosive detonated in Boston," the reporter said. "Do you think the President has handled this series of events well?"

"There was a second attack?" Claire asked in horror.

"Well," another voice on the radio chimed in, "I think the decision to shut down all borders and cancel all flights coming in and out of the United States has many people fearing the worst."

"Closed the border?" Claire asked.

"I don't necessarily think he has handled anything wrong. It's really tough, to be honest. The decision is a big one, but I am not sure he had much choice. There have been mass quantities of deadly chemicals stolen from a highly experimental lab followed by the *two* biggest attacks on the United States. All in the same day."

"Honey?" Claire said.

"He is trying to take back control," the reporter went on, "The military is patrolling, and martial law is being enforced. Cities and neighborhoods will be on lockdown. The President and the United States government are trying to settle everyone down and take back control. There is way too much tension in the country right now, and I think we can all agree on that. It's a difficult situation, and we just need to get through the rest of the day and greet tomorrow with open arms."

"Honey?" Claire repeated.

Mark realized he was drifting into the other lane and corrected his steering.

"How about that music, Dad?" James asked.

Claire turned the dial for him. Static. Static. Static. Classical piano.

"I didn't mean this," James insisted.

Mark turned up the volume, but it was the news reporters occupying his mind. They all spoke over one another, as if debating which part was worse. Deadly chemicals. Mass fatalities. Martial law. Closed borders. Mark Frasier. His conscience was dragged through the guilt with nothing to hide behind.

Mark stared straight ahead and did everything he could to hold back the tears he wished to spill out. He needed to remain calm. For them.

Static. Claire changed the channel and looked at her husband, as if she could feel the way his thoughts clawed at his brain. Static. Static. Soft rock. The vocalist sang over the laid-back beat.

"Here you go, James," Claire stated.

"Thanks, Mom."

Claire turned it up. "I always liked this one."

Mark kept his eyes forward. James nodded his head to the drums. Kelsey copied her older brother, and even Claire tapped her foot.

They all tried to forget.

The snow picked up again.

The singer's voice blurred and morphed. He sang a different tune, but only for Mark.

"Mark Frasier never cared for anyone. Mark Frasier only cared for himself. Mark Frasier killed thousands of people to save himself and his family.

Mark Frasier, Mark Frasier, Mark Frasier. And no one else matters."

He gripped the wheel tighter.

"Mark Frasier is a selfish man who helped bring the entire nation to its knees. Mark Frasier will hide in the frozen depths of Canada while families back in America mourn and suffer. Mark Frasier, Mark Frasier, Mark Frasier. And no one else matters."

Mark shut off the radio.

"What'd you do that for?" James asked.

"I don't like that song," he replied.

"What are you talking about?" Claire asked. "You love that song."

"Not anymore."

The air in the van was stale and awkward. Despite the snow, Claire cracked her window open to let in some fresh air.

Night came closer. 5:24 pm.

THE TRAFFIC

Another set of helicopters flew overhead in a northerly direction. The snow endured and the sky darkened as the sun neared the horizon. 5:38 pm.

They passed another sign.

CANADA 5 MILES.

Mark panicked, but he tried not to show it. He could never show it. How much time did he have? How much longer could they keep this up? At least he felt like a father again, at least a little. He held on to it like a lost memory suddenly remembered.

He looked over to Claire, and she looked back. A smile brightened her face, but it seemed artificial. She was still being supportive, but the doubt in her face was obvious. In all of their faces, especially his.

Traffic ahead. Traffic at a dead stop.

Mark pulled up behind the last car and hoped it passed quickly. The car in front was packed to the brim with containers poorly strapped to the roof.

"Do you think?" Claire asked.

Mark switched the gear to reverse but another car pulled up close behind them. It was jam-packed too.

"Great." Mark lifted his hands in the air. "How about a little room, buddy?" Another car pulled in behind that one and then another. No one was budging, and they all seemed prepared for a sudden and permanent move.

Mark used the couple of feet he had to maneuver into the other lane. It was a nine-point escape. He drove in the opposite lane, but still headed north.

"Honey…" Claire said. "What are you doing?"

"Looking for the next turn," he replied. "All these people are in line waiting to go into Canada, right? Eh?" he said in an atrocious Canadian accent. "And you heard the radio. The borders are closed. This line isn't moving. I'm not cutting them off if I plan to turn. These people just don't know that yet. That's why they're upset."

"What if there is no turn?" Claire rebutted.

"In five miles? Hard to believe."

"What does that mean for *us*?"

"Don't worry." Mark kept his gaze ahead.

The other vehicles beeped and honked. Some held down their horns longer than others. Some even yelled out their windows with shaking fists.

"Look," Mark said, "an intersection."

He turned and connected onto the other road and headed west. The road navigated into the northern woods.

"Good thing we didn't make a scene," Claire said.

The car traveled deeper and deeper into the woods while Mark traveled deeper and deeper into his memories. He repeated the last six years of his life. The six years he spent as an employee of Valine Corp.

Where did it all go wrong?

The sun dipped behind the tall pines and the snow continued. 5:47 pm.

THE WOODS

The woods darkened and night took over. Snow-covered cedar, pine and birch offered brilliant scenery in the headlights. He flicked on the brights and visibility exploded, but only on one side. The other bulb must be dead.

A fork in the road lay ahead. Mark veered right, and the paved road turned to what felt like gravel under snow. Then gravel to dirt. Then the dirt road to a bumpier, narrower, dirtier one. It was all slow-moving, but there were no other cars in sight.

Mark spiraled back into his mind. The men with rifles. Sulfuric Nine. The cops. What was going to happen next? What were they going to do in Canada?

The wipers scraped against the windshield, and he came back to the present. The snow had stopped, or at least the canopy of branches above protected them well. Either way, Mark was glad.

He quickly sank back into his thoughts. What if this road did not even lead into Canada? He looked at the bottom corner of the rearview mirror, where a digital reading displayed *NW*. It must lead into Canada. A deep breath. They must be close.

"You sure you know where you're going?" Claire asked, right on cue.

"Yes."

"This road leads into Canada?"

"It's still going north, so it must."

"Northwest."

"Yeah, north."

The right front wheel slammed into a pothole and then back out again. It shook the whole van and everyone in it. It was rough for both passengers and vehicle, but they passed the obstacle and drove on.

"Can you turn up the heat?" Kelsey asked, so Claire did. The temperature was dropping outside, but at least the snow had stopped, Mark reminded himself. He repeated it over and over. It was the glowing positive in the giant heap of burning garbage. 6:41 pm.

"We passed the five-mile sign about an hour ago, right?" James asked.

"Sure, something like that," Mark replied.

"Then we traveled what? A mile, maybe more, past the traffic before turning?"

"Yeah." Mark began to see where his train of thought was going.

"That leaves, let's say, three to four miles. If the first road we turned on paralleled the border and then this second road travels northwest… this road is much slower, windier, and the route longer, but we must have been driving on this road for what? Forty minutes?"

"I think you're right, son." Mark loved his son's mathematically inclined brain. He got it from him.

"One mile tops, if you ask me," James concluded. "One mile to Canada."

"And then what?" Claire asked.

"I said we'll figure it out when we get there." Mark still had no idea. Not even a clue.

Relieve all the stress, my friend. Relieve all the tension and move on with your life. Move on to a good life. Your new life.

"Hello? Earth to Mark?" Claire was still talking. His lack of plan had been eating away at her all day, and she finally demanded more. "Less than one mile to Canada. Then what?"

Mark looked into the rearview mirror to see James comforting Kelsey. "Can we talk about this later?"

"What about tonight?" she asked.

"Tonight?" Mark gazed ahead as far into the woods as the headlights touched. "There's camping stuff in the back."

"Camping stuff?" She laughed and looked out the window. "We've never camped before, but now we're going to camp in snow?"

"We've camped before."

"What? Before the kids, twenty years ago?"

"We won't even need to sleep outside. The van is plenty big. The kids can stretch out in the back."

"Living in a stolen van in Canada for the rest of our lives." Claire was beginning to sound like James.

"Just for the night."

"For many nights. What if bombs keep going off all over the country?"

"I… I…"

"We can't go out in public. We can't go to the cops. We can't go back to our own country. What are we really going to do, Mark?"

"We will figure it out."

"You've been saying that all day. I'm sick of it."

"Please, Claire!" Mark snapped. "We have made it all the way to the Canadian border. Henry and his family didn't even make it to lunch."

There was a long silence. Mark questioned why he brought up his dead coworker and family. It was the only comparison he could think of.

And they were dead.

Another set of headlights came their way. They were much closer together and did not appear to be a car.

"Mark…"

The road was narrow and the snow was built up on the sides. Mark moved onto the bank and into deeper snow to make enough space for the other vehicle to pass. Branches scratched against the side of the van and more snow fell onto the roof.

It was a snowmobile, and the man waved with enthusiasm. Mark returned the favor and they passed without incident.

Mark steered back onto the road from the bank, but the back tires dropped into a stubborn patch. The tires struggled for traction on the ice under the snow. The tires spun like a treadmill too fast to land a foot on. The old rubber had little left in it.

The snowmobiler noticed and turned around.

Mark watched him in the side mirror.

He sighed and switched off his headlights to

allow darkness to swallow the van.

The snowmobiler approached the driver's-side window and removed his helmet. He knocked lightly on the glass with gloves.

"What are you going to do *now*?" Claire asked.

Mark tried the pedal again. The tires spun on the ice, and the van shifted in place. The snowmobiler jumped back with his arms in the air.

Mark lowered his window.

"Hey, man, not cool," the rider said.

"I'm sorry," Mark replied.

"I was just seeing if you needed help, man. Looks like you're stuck."

"I am stuck. Can you help?"

"Yeah, I can. Do you have rope?"

"I think so. In the back." He found Claire's glance before leaving the van.

Mark realized his face was exposed, but the man seemed none the wiser. It was dark with only the snowmobile headlights, and the two of them walked to the back of the van. Mark searched through the bag for the coiled rope he had seen earlier and pulled it out.

"Name's Corey." The man held out a hand.

Mark hesitated and then shook. "Gary."

"I'll get the sled and we'll pull you right out." Corey hopped on the snowmobile and positioned it in front of the old van. "Killer van by the way."

Mark climbed underneath the bumper and tied the rope several times over onto the frame of the vehicle. The knots were secured, and he brought the other end for Corey to tie onto the back of the snowmobile.

"I'll follow your lead... so to speak." Corey laughed and put on his helmet. He revved up the snowmobile and offered a thumbs-up.

Mark stepped back into the van.

"He didn't recognize you?"

"I don't think so."

Mark slammed on the pedal. The tires spun out of control. Corey kicked off the brake and pulled the rope. The van tires scraped the underlying ice and struggled, but the snowmobile was built for these conditions and had superb traction.

The van slowly moved from the deeper bank and back onto the narrow road. The tires finally gripped and the van escaped.

Mark hastily stepped out and untied the rope from the frame as fast as possible. Corey turned around and rode over.

"Right on, man!" he said. "What are you guys doing out here anyway? Avoiding the lines?" He chuckled as he stepped off his snowmobile.

"How'd you guess?"

"That's what I would do. World's gone crazy, man. Or at least this country."

"You can say that again," Mark said as the stubborn knot loosened. "So we're still in America?"

"Not in Canada yet."

"Where do you live?" Mark pulled his head from underneath the van and straight into the headlights of the newly positioned snowmobile.

It struck Corey like a bat to the head. He had not recognized him because of the dark. But now. Now he recognized Mark, and it was plain to see on his face.

"Whoa!" Corey stumbled backward. "No, no, no…"

Mark jumped to his feet and held out his hands. "Corey… I'm innocent. We're innocent. We were set up, and we can't go to the police. You have to believe me."

Corey glanced over to his snowmobile.

"Corey," Mark said, "let's talk about this. Please."

Corey looked again to his sled and sprinted for it.

"I have a gun!" Mark shouted.

BANG.

He fired it in the air and the sound echoed through the empty woods. Kelsey could be heard screaming in the van, but Mark did not dare gaze over.

Corey stopped and turned slowly. Mark approached him and saw the fear in his eyes. It made him ashamed to be aiming the weapon, but he had no choice. Again.

"Let's talk about this," Mark said.

Corey stared at the handgun with his arms up and offered no reply.

"I was forced to steal the Sulfuric Nine. We had guns to our heads. I had nothing to do with the bombs."

More silence.

"Please, you have to believe me. Do not go to the cops. I have a family."

"Everyone has a family," Corey added.

"You have kids?"

"No."

"Then you don't understand."

Corey pushed Mark into the snow and tried disarming him.

BANG.

Corey collapsed in the snow.

A red stain spread on his jacket. He tried holding it in with his gloved hands but it spilled onto the white snow.

Mark stared with eyes wide open as the pistol shook in his hands and smoke left the barrel.

Corey tried speaking but only coughed up blood. The red stain in the snow grew around his entire body as his strength ebbed by the second.

Mark finally gazed back to the van. Claire gawked as James comforted a hysterical Kelsey. Tears rolled down all three faces.

What had he done? What had he become?

He looked back to Corey. He was dead.

Mark dropped the gun in the snow as if no one had seen it and stepped back to the van, focusing on each foot. One stepping in front of the other. His hands shook like he was seconds from frostbite. His heart pounded and his forehead was soaked with a nervous sweat.

The snow and woods felt like a dream.

A nightmare.

He opened the door and quietly sat down in the driver's seat. Not a single word from anyone. Only the crying and wiping of tears. His family looked more scared than ever, and he felt it was directed at him.

Mark turned the keys and shifted. He tried to

ignore the blood and the death, but snuck a last glance at the body to remind himself what he was now, if not before.

A murderer.

The Frasiers carried on northwest. 6:58 pm.

THE CAMPSITE

They drove in absolute silence for three slow miles until the glow of a small town revealed itself in the night. 7:33 pm.

The town rested along a wide river. The river had to be the St. Lawrence River, the border separating the two countries. The town was on the Canadian side and they were still on the American side.

"There it is." He hoped someone else would break the agonizing silence, but he could no longer take it. It needed to be done. He needed to shift his thoughts from Corey before they completely consumed him.

He stopped the van for a moment. The wooded hill sloped down and offered a great view of the town lower in the valley. The moon was bright and the stars were out.

He pressed on the gas again and followed the road deeper into the woods. The silence wore on as the tires crunched through snow and ice.

An open pocket in the thick woods seemed perfect for the van to settle. It was not far off the road but well hidden. Not that anyone would be driving up this way. Or maybe they would. What did Mark know? 7:51 pm.

"I spy… the perfect campsite," Mark said, but no one played. He parked and shut off the headlights.

Darkness took over.

"What do you think?" he asked.

"Here?" Claire replied.

"For the night."

"Good as any, I suppose."

Mark stepped outside. It was colder than he thought. The air had a bite to it, so he zipped up his jacket and wrapped the red scarf around his neck.

He opened the bag in the van and pulled out all the items. He spread everything out and took inventory. Tent, two sleeping bags, two blankets, a sweatshirt, a towel, a folding knife, three carabiners, a flashlight, a box of matches, a dozen zip ties, a container of doggy poop bags, and a second set of coiled rope.

It was the jackpot. But no food and no water.

Mark's stomach growled. Their breakfast was hours ago and he was feeling it. He hated going to sleep on an empty stomach. He also hated being a murderer.

SNAP.

A stick broke in the quiet forest. He flicked on the flashlight and pointed it at the darkness of the woods. Nothing but the night. Another deep breath.

HOOT.

An owl startled him. He shined the light on the creature perched on a nearby branch, but it flew away.

Mark powered down the flashlight and threw it with the other stuff.

Murderer.

He grabbed the bag and closed the back doors. Then he noticed the sky. The moon and the stars were brilliant out here with so little light pollution. He could see Orion's Belt and the Little Dipper. Both were so clear and vivid, he almost smiled.

He knocked on the van and the doors opened. Claire stepped out first, then James and Kelsey. They rubbed their arms and hands for warmth. Their eyes wandered all around, everywhere but on him. It was a dagger to the chest.

"Look." Mark pointed up. The sheer number of glowing dots in the night sky was intoxicating, but only to Mark. It reminded him of happier times as a child when he wished to be an astronaut. He remembered it so well, but it was more practical to be a chemist.

Chemistry. Sulfuric Nine. Corey.

Mark showed them all the ones he knew, which was a good many. The North Star, Orion, Scorpius, Cassiopeia, Draco, Capricornus, Sagittarius, and on and on.

No one asked questions, and they received the lesson as if forced. Their minds were distracted.

Their father was a murderer.

"Come on," he said, "let's go back inside." He distributed the gear to his family. The children received a sleeping bag each while the parents got blankets. Kelsey was given the sweatshirt and James the flashlight. The rest of the stuff was put in the middle for grabs.

There was a long silence.

"I'm hungry," Kelsey said, and James nudged her, as if saying anything was a bad idea.

"I know, honey." Mark was glad to hear her soft voice. "It may have to stay like that until the morning."

A single thought overwhelmed him, and he felt a certainty about it. A chance to redeem himself.

But from murder?

"Unless…" Mark pulled out the rope, and everyone looked at one another with great concern. "Unless I can set traps. A bit thick for traps but maybe it'll do."

"Traps?" Claire asked sarcastically. "You're going to set traps?"

"Yes."

"What do you know about setting traps?"

"How hard could it be? We're surrounded by snow. It'll be easy to find tracks. See where they like to go. Isn't that what you do? Set the traps in high-traffic areas?"

"What do you plan on trapping?"

"I don't know… a rabbit?"

"How are you going to cook it?"

"We have matches, don't we? Plenty of firewood."

"Okay, Bear Grylls." Claire sighed and gazed out the window.

"Can I have the flashlight, James?" Mark turned the engine back on and looked to Claire. "Keep it warm for me, okay?"

She looked at him with raised eyebrows. "Okay."

He grabbed the rope and flashlight and exited the van at 8:17 pm. He trekked away, but someone followed. It was Claire, and she caught up.

"What the hell, Mark?" she asked.

"What?"

"You killed a man."

"Accidently! He attacked me."

"You held a gun to him."

"He was going to…"

"I'm sorry," Claire interrupted.

"For what, honey?"

"I'm sorry for not talking you out of that job." She gazed deep into his eyes. "I'm sorry for a lot of things."

"Me too."

Claire kissed him on the lips. It was gentle yet firm. She looked back into his eyes like when they were first dating. It filled him with warmth. She knew he was only doing this for them and there was no going to the cops now. But she did not look angry, only accepting. She fell in love with the money even more than him. The whole family did.

"Let me help with the traps."

"No, it's fine, really. I can handle this."

"Are you sure?"

"Yes. Stay with the kids. They need their mother. I'm afraid you're their last real parent."

"Don't say that."

"I'm a murderer, Claire. How could they look at me any differently? I can already see it on their faces. They're afraid to even speak to me."

"Just come back with some rabbits."

"That's not how trapping works."

"Like you would know?" Claire scurried to the warmth of the van.

Mark looked back to the thick woods. He shined the flashlight ahead, and the night swallowed the dim light. He carefully moved through the snowy terrain in search of animal tracks.

He studied the rope again. It was far too thick to catch small game. The critters would see it easily. Even he knew that. But he had to try. For them.

Mark gazed back in the direction of the van. The distant engine could be heard but he could no longer see it.

He marched deeper into the woods.

He remembered a documentary he watched about modern-day fur trappers. They checked dozens of traps and would still sometimes get nothing. Dozens of traps. It would be easier if he had the same equipment. They used snowmobiles.

Snowmobiles. Corey.

He could see Corey's face. It was seared into his memory and overpowered him. He could see his face falling apart piece by piece like crumbling stone from an ancient cathedral. Mark shook the image from his head. For now.

SNAP.

Mark flashed the light in the direction of the sound. Then in every direction. But there was nothing to see, so he kept hiking.

The whistling wind and rattling branches of nearby pines made him uneasy. His wandering mind did nothing to help. He no longer felt like a father. The thing that had kept him going all day. He was a murderer now, and that's all his children would ever see.

SNAP.

A branch cracked and collapsed in the empty woods. He turned and sprinted toward the van.

He remembered the rope in his hand and tossed it away. He fumbled the door handle of the van and jumped inside, nearly out of breath.

"What was all that about?" Claire asked.

"There was… It was… cold."

"You set the traps?"

"Yup."

"Well, that was fast."

"Nothing to it."

"How many did you set?"

"Four. One. Just one."

"Just one?"

"I'm very confident in it."

Mark and Claire found each other's eyes. They looked deeply into one another. Then a pile of snow dumped onto the hood from a nearby branch. It startled everyone, especially Mark.

"I think we should all get some sleep," he said. "It's after eight thirty, and we've all been up since very early this morning."

"You're right," Claire agreed. "We'll get a good night's sleep and tackle tomorrow with clear minds."

He smiled back. "Thank you."

Mark and Claire wrapped themselves in blankets and adjusted their seats as best they could for sleeping. The children lay in the back in the sleeping bags, whispering to one another.

Mark wished he could hear what they were

saying, but he knew.

He turned off the engine, but his mind still roared on. Memories and memories. Corey's death. The deaths of thousands. And more scenarios. Scenarios of tomorrow. Of the rest of their lives.

Sleep became a distant thought as time ticked on.

"How about a bedtime story?" Claire suggested.

"A bedtime story?" Mark asked.

She nodded and placed her hand on his. Mark searched for one in the back of his crowded mind.

"Bedtime story…" he repeated. "Let me think, let me think. Oh yeah, that's a good one. Have you ever heard of *The Giving Tree* by Shel Silverstein?"

Kelsey shook her head. James moved his eyes to the window.

"I can't believe I've never read you that one," he said. "It was a favorite of mine growing up, and it's always stuck with me, even to this day. Now, I don't have it memorized, but I think I can do it justice. And it starts with a young boy and an old tree who were good friends."

THE NIGHT

Mark could not sleep. How could he? How could he ever sleep again? He did well to convince himself that the thousands of deaths were not on him. Not his fault. The terrorists were the ones responsible. He was forced to do what he did, used like a pawn. Not even a pawn. Those men were going to kill his family.

But Corey. He was different, and Mark knew that better than anyone. He murdered him in cold blood.

He purchased the gun.

He loaded the gun.

He fired the gun.

Mark adjusted his seat to an upright position. Claire slept comfortably in her blanket beside him. James and Kelsey were snuggled in their sleeping bags. The three of them had passed out almost instantly. It was a long day. He turned on the engine for warmth. 10:44 pm.

Claire shifted and opened her eyes.

"Just warming up the van, honey," he said. "Go back to sleep."

She clutched her blanket tightly around her

shoulders and closed her eyes. Mark watched and felt a crippling sadness that he had never felt before. A sadness that was rooted in his heart and blossomed in his soul.

A sadness that tore him apart.

He turned the heat up. It felt nice on his skin. It was damn cold out, and he wanted to be as warm as possible before stepping outside.

He was going to walk to town.

His time was up. He was going to face the charges. The terrorists would not find him in a small Canadian river town. He would be fine and report everything he knew. It was not much, but it was something.

If he did this, and only if he did this, would his family have a chance to live a life vaguely resembling a normal one. Not one on the run. He owed his family that much. They had stuck by him this far. Bless them.

The van heated up quickly.

Mark heated up quickly.

This was it. He gazed over to Claire. Her face was so gorgeous in the moonlight. The same could be said about Kelsey and James.

They were all so beautiful.

They were the only things he truly loved. Not the job, not the money, not the house. It was his family, and that was agonizingly clear now.

A tear rolled down his cheek as he turned the engine off. He might never see them again. No, he would, just not for a while. He searched the center console for something to write on.

He found a napkin and a pen. He wanted to

write a million things, to pour his heart out like a poet, but he settled on three words.

I LOVE YOU.

He placed the napkin on the driver's seat and opened the door.

"Where are you going?" Claire mumbled.

"I have to pee," he replied. "I'll just be a minute."

Claire placed her head back down, and the children rolled into different positions.

Mark watched them all one last time before closing the door and entering the frozen night.

10:52 pm.

It was windy and chilly. He rubbed his hands together and wrapped the blanket around his body.

Mark trekked back the way they drove, but the van door opened, and it stopped him in his tracks.

Kelsey had slipped out of her sleeping bag and approached.

"Daddy?" She rubbed her exhausted eyes.

Mark's tongue was tied.

"Where are you going?"

"Bathroom," he finally said. "Just going to the bathroom, sweetie. Go back inside before you catch a cold." His eyes were filling with tears.

Kelsey wrapped her small arms around him and squeezed tightly, as if she knew what was happening. As if, only for a second, she had forgotten what he had done and wholeheartedly accepted him as her father. He cried.

"Why are you crying, Daddy?"

"It's just the cold," he lied. "Now go back inside and warm up. I will be right back. I promise."

Why did he add that last part? He hated himself for it. He hated himself for many things, but being a poor father topped the list. He watched young Kelsey climb back into the van and close the door.

He hoped he was making the right choice.

He turned and walked on. For them.

The snow was deep and he made slow progress. He turned back to the van one last time but could no longer see it. It vanished in the night.

He cried harder, but the tears froze on his face in the wind. Memories of his family swept in and pushed out the darker stuff. But it was always temporary.

His mind always reverted back to Corey and what he had done. What he needed to do.

THE COST

Mark hiked on. He hiked for what seemed like a lifetime. The wind rolled through the roadway, and the temperature dropped with every step.

He checked his gold watch. 11:41 pm.

He wondered if he could make it. He wondered if he had made the right choice. He would be no good if he collapsed and died in the snow. Buried and frozen. He clutched onto the blanket and tucked his face inside.

The illumination of the Canadian river town came into view. The river ran alongside the town, but there was no bridge in sight.

Mark looked down the wooded hill with tired eyes. He felt the warmth and allure of the lights below. He truly felt them. Or perhaps it was the sense of doing the right thing in giving himself up.

He wanted to believe in both, so he did.

He trekked down the hill one cold step at a time. Snowdrift piled up to his knees as he trudged down the windy slope. He fell and stumbled. He got up and kept going. He fell again. Got up and kept going again.

He made it down the hill and onto flat ground,

then onto the stretch near the riverbank. The river he must cross to get to the town. To save his family. He chose not to think about his shivering body and focused only on them.

Claire, James and Kelsey. The three things that mattered in life. The three.

Suddenly, there they were. They all smiled and waved in front of him, looking warm in thick winter jackets.

He collapsed to his knees. It couldn't be.

Kelsey encouraged her father to join them where they stood. Her brother rested his hand on her shoulder, and Claire signaled for him to hurry. He did not have much time.

The whole family was glowing with enthusiasm. They wanted their father back.

Mark pulled himself from the snow and trekked toward them. With each step, they seemed to move farther and farther away, so he hastened his pace.

"Come on!" they shouted and waved him on.

A snowflake dropped on his nose. Another on his eyebrow. The snow returned and with it increased winds, increased shivering.

His family disappeared, blowing away like dust too thin to grab hold of.

He plunged into the St. Lawrence River.

The splash was loud and the struggle furious. The bitter cold soaked his clothes and chilled him down to the bone. He lost the blanket and fought the current as it dragged him downriver.

The lights of the town drifted away.

He tried swimming. He tried everything. His frozen arms paddled and his legs kicked. Every inch of his body screamed in numbing pain. Movement became harder and harder, slower and slower. He shook at an alarming rate, and his limbs became warm.

His whole body began burning up.

He managed to see his watch. It had stopped working in the cold water of the great river.

The hands were stuck at midnight.

Music played in the distance. It was faint but soon sharpened.

Mark opened his eyes and stood before a wooden table set for dinner. His family surrounded him with hungry stomachs and smiling faces.

It was six years ago. James was his sister's age and Kelsey much younger. The music was loud and clear now.

It was Christmas music.

Only the tune and crudely decorated pine tree in the corner suggested the time of year. No other decorations, no centerpiece, no tablecloth, no placemats.

Mark looked down to see a fork in one hand and a serving knife in the other. He cut a meager roast chicken while Claire poured cheap wine. The smells were amazing.

"Looks delicious," James said.

"You can thank your mother for that," Mark replied.

"Not *all* the thanks." Claire passed the small bowl of corn to her son after scooping a spoonful onto Kelsey's plate. "Even you mashed the potatoes, James."

"How much does everyone want?" Mark

paused his carving.

"A lot!" Kelsey demanded with a plastic fork and spoon in each hand and a bib waiting to be dirtied.

The family laughed.

"Well, there's not much." Mark slid the entire chicken her way.

"I'll take one full chicken as well, please," James added. More laughter.

Mark finished carving and distributed pieces onto each plate. The peas and mashed potatoes were passed around too, and the family settled in the creaky chairs before diving in.

Mark found Claire's eyes across the table, and they both smiled. She offered her hands for James and Kelsey to hold and Mark did the same. They closed their eyes and bowed their heads.

"Bless us, O Lord," Mark said, "and these, Thy gifts, which we are about to receive from Thy bounty. Through Christ, our Lord. Amen."

"Amen," the others said.

"And Merry Christmas!" Kelsey shouted.

"And Merry Christmas," Mark said.

"Dig in!" Claire said. And they did.

The chicken was devoured. The corn destroyed. The peas gobbled. The mashed potatoes ravaged. The family had satisfied bellies and smiles on their faces.

Mark watched. He watched Kelsey fling a pea at her brother and James fling one back. He watched his wife tell them off but eventually join in too. He watched his family be happy and enjoy one another's company.

He watched love.

He looked around. The house was old and needed many repairs. Things were cluttered everywhere because the space was so small. The rickety shelves across the wall housed the many photos of great family memories, but the shelf looked ready to fall with another ounce of weight.

"Hey, James," Mark said. "Do you want to play baseball this spring?"

His son's eyes lit up. "What?"

"Do you want to play baseball?"

"Yes!"

"Merry Christmas. How about you, Kelsey? Do you want to sign up for ballet?"

"Yes!" she answered with even more enthusiasm.

"Merry Christmas." Mark found Claire's eyes once again.

She looked concerned. "You think the interview went *that* well?"

"I don't know," Mark said. "Do you want a new car? Something that starts more than half the time."

"Mark, let's be serious."

"The interview went very well, Claire, and I have the degrees Valine Corp needs. I'd be shocked not to get a position. What color car do you want?"

"I just don't know about the company, Mark."

"It will be fine, honey. The money will convince you. Merry Christmas."

Everything went BLACK.

We understand the cost in our hearts
When fog rolls in and covers the sea
Studied all the maps and all the charts
We just needed the time to be free

Spirits collapse and most turn back
Simple paths were never promised
Learning and evading the next attack
In the depths of the empty honest

Tread against wind and dried leaves
Crunching underneath boots in silence
Flesh remains separate and grieves
Stand and wait for the gentle sirens

Wet the stone and grip the handle
Grind the tired edge back and forth
Using the light of a single candle
Reunion in south but facing north

Witness glories fall and never rise
How the cold bites deep and numbs
Far beyond the screams and the cries
Listen with care for unending drums

To See

Mahpiya opened her eyes one morning and was blind. She had known it was coming for a while now and felt lucky to have held on to her sight for sixty-six winters.

Better than most.

But this was it. Total and absolute blackness. It curled around her and gripped tightly. There would be no escaping it, not this time, but she knew the layout of the tipi, and the camp stayed much the same even when it moved.

So she replaced the darkness with the familiar and started with the fire pit. The heart of the tipi, of any home. Then the several large stones confining it to the center. The few burnt logs and pile of ash from last night's fire lingered. She'd awoken to the sight so many times, it was so easy to imagine.

She looked up to where she knew the dreamcatcher was hanging from a wooden beam. It swayed gently back and forth as heavy gusts from the open plains battered the outside of the buffalo skin walls. Stitched together with great skill, several tanned hides sheltered her from the howling wind she could hear so clearly.

She focused on it and nothing else.

When she opened her eyes, a new scene appeared.

The endless grasslands of the wide-open plains surrounded her as she rode bareback on a white-and-brown horse. She was younger, much younger, no more than fourteen winters. And her eyes worked perfectly.

She embraced the wind blowing through her thick black hair. The rolling hills, whistling winds and waving grass dominated her senses.

It was the feeling of freedom, and she savored it. Only her horse offered such a thing, and she loved him for it. She leaned forward and kicked her heels to hasten the pace.

Her eyes widened. The horse tried stopping but only collapsed brutally in the effort. She and her horse stumbled into a large hole that dropped fifteen feet into a jagged cave.

They fell, and they fell hard.

Mahpiya's left wrist snapped, and a knock to the head made her woozy. The pain was so intense, it stopped feeling like pain at all. She tried holding her wrist together with her other hand but could not bear to look.

She limited her vomit to a swallowed mouthful and a few leaked drops onto the cave floor.

But there was only one thing grinding her attention.

The deathly whimpering and neighing of her horse. She gazed over to see all four legs broken. He kicked and struggled as his snapped bones oozed with blood. A sharp rock had punctured his stomach and ribs too. The blood trailed through cracks and crevices in the rock floor before pooling near Mahpiya.

Tears rolled down her cheeks as she limped over and unsheathed a small blade. The harsh cries from the dying steed pierced her ears and forced her eyes closed, as if what she did not see did not happen.

The knife did the job, and silence took over.

But then her own cries filled the small cave. They worsened when she looked up to the sky. It was presented to her in a frame of slick cave walls. The wind was blowing overhead.

She looked back to the cave walls. The steep rock appeared unclimbable even with two good wrists. She pressed her hand against the rock. It was cold and slimy. She moved her fingers along the wall, hoping the strange surface would offer a solution.

Then she saw it. A small crevice in the rock. It led to complete darkness, and she would have to crawl on her stomach. And with one wrist. But it was hope.

The bright blue sky drew her attention again. It looked so lovely. The warm sun and the cool breeze. The wind swept around, and the grasses danced for their only audience.

She looked back to the crevice. It was the only way. She lowered herself onto the rocky floor and winced. Her wrist screamed and her head pounded.

The crevice seemed even smaller now, but she could still fit, and she carefully pushed herself forward with her feet and right arm. The patches of light behind her faded quickly, and darkness took over.

The utter darkness found only in caves where eyes never adjust. Even if she was down here for days, weeks, they would never adjust.

One thought suddenly poured into her mind and filled it to the top. She would be unable to brag to her brothers about the wolf she had seen on her ride that evening.

A beautiful gray wolf, alone but healthy. White fur started at the stomach and darkened as it rose over its back and shoulders and ears. He did not show his teeth, and Mahpiya was glad.

They found one another's eyes instead, and she discovered the first similarity. Both their eyes were blue. Then a second. They were both scared.

She smiled, and then the wolf darted off. The moment was over. She smacked herself when she realized what she had done. She had shown *her* teeth.

But now the memory might die with her in this cave. A story meant to be told. So she crawled and she crawled.

The crevice eventually widened, but the darkness was here to stay.

She stood up with wobbly knees and a guiding right hand, but nearly choked on the stench of dank, musty rock.

She moved her right hand back and forth, up and down, and then she walked forward. Still no sign of the jagged walls. A few more steps. Still nothing.

Noises of fluttering wings overhead consumed

her, and she stopped. The disturbance of a visitor seemed to have riled something up. Flying and swooping all around. She could feel the breeze of the passing flights.

Bats.

She dropped to the cave floor and banged her broken wrist on a rock. Her scream was so loud and so violent that every single bat quickly found a place to settle and remained.

She cried and she cried.

Pain had never felt so real.

She closed her eyes tight and tried blocking it all out. The cave, her horse, her wrist, the bats. It was all just a nightmare. Her dreamcatcher was not working.

She opened her eyes, and everything was still.

The infinite blackness was there, the sobbing heart remained, the shooting pain too, but no more bats. Silence filled her ears, but deep in the back of her mind she knew the truth. They were still there. Hanging and watching.

She remembered the gray wolf and all of its allure. She remembered him so well that she could see him in front of her so vividly.

Their eyes met once more. They were even bluer than she remembered, underneath bright white eyebrows. His jet-black nose gave way to black lips and a gray snout and white chin. The beautiful creature turned and strolled away.

But this time, he moved slow enough for her to follow. He even turned his head once or twice to see if she was coming.

Mahpiya gave chase and forgot about waving

her arm in front of her. She was quickly reminded by a hard wall and painful grimace.

And the wolf was gone.

She touched the jagged, slimy rock and moved her fingers across it. She stepped along the wall and continued feeling around the cave, shuffling her feet faster and faster as the bats stirred once more.

Soon many were back in flight, diving and soaring. She ignored it, kept focused on her task.

Then she saw it.

A faint light pierced the darkness. She followed it, faster and faster.

The light suddenly burst into a much brighter one.

She was transported back to the present. Back inside the comfort of her tipi.

Eager children rushed inside, and she wished she could see the enthusiasm on all their faces.

"Unci! Unci!" a few shouted.

"Yes, yes. My little ones." She crossed her legs and rubbed her left wrist. It had healed long ago, but it had never been the same. "What is it?"

"You never finished the story!"

Her smile widened from ear to ear. A smile reserved for special occasions. Like the wolf in the cave, she realized she did not need to see with her eyes to observe the light. It filled her body and warmed her heart.

The source was her grandchildren.

The source was the love of stories.

The source was all around her.

"Would you like me to start from the beginning?"